Sisters at the Edge of the World

Ailish Sinclair

GRAUPIUS

For Davie

The End

The God stands before me. Me. Morragh, who never speaks.

And I speak.

Who would have thought that my silence would ever come to an end, let alone in such a glorious and loud way.

At first I sing. I sing to Him. It is so easy. It just flows out of me. The tales of my life become music. The wonderment of the world is song. The delight in the curve of a leaf and the swoop of a bird in flight make bright notes in my throat. I have sung here before, of course. Within the sacred Circle. But it has never sounded like this. I have always been alone. Unheard. Tonight the song seems to dance round the space, to bounce in excitement, and then slow as if for a caress. Each tall stone, and the large recumbent, are topped with wee piles of snow and these reverberate with music. I see the snow shake. I feel the vibration of the stones too. They make the sound rich and sonorous, as if my voice were more than one.

It is my wonderment and delight in Him that is expressed. That is the cause of the change in sound, the real difference here. The God is not as depicted and described in the stories of my people. He is come as he has appeared to others from far away, so he looks like them. There is the scent of far-off places on him. Strange foods and oils and smoke. He is like a traveller. An adventurer.

The feet of a bear lie between Him and me. Two prints in the snow, huge and clawed, like their maker. I knew she had been here when I arrived earlier; I sensed her musk in the cold air. My great friend, my Mother Bear. She did not wait to meet me today as she sometimes does in the forest, though this meeting is no less portentous because we did not encounter one another face to face. At first I thought her presence here was what was different, what was to be special about this night.

But no.

It is this.

It is Him.

He kneels before me. My feet are now standing in the bear prints, legs wide as I speak on and on, seemingly unable to stem the flow of words, and I study the details of the God. He does not mind if I touch. My fingers feel leather and woven cloth, metal hidden within. He is a mix of our earthly substances. But his face is flesh. Like a man. Just like a man. His nose is long and pleasing to look at. His eyes, the only eyes I have ever looked directly into, are dark and have seen many far off places, all the places of the earth.

And the sky.

And the sea.

He looks straight back at me too. He smiles into my eyes, into my heart, into the whole of my being, and then my exploring hands find his belt and the metal that is hidden there. He gives the knife to me, holding it out like an offering. I take it and touch it to my face, my cheek, my mouth. Then I hand it back. It is not for me to keep, this knife of a God. I pull the swirled dragon band off my wrist and hand it to him. It is the only adornment I wear this night, and it is the most valuable jewellery I own. It is what should be presented to Him. He studies it. He approves. But, like me, he gives it back. He pushes it up over my hand and onto my arm where it belongs.

And it is then, as I feel the touch of his fingers on my arm and on my hand, that I understand why he is come as a man to me. I take his hands and lead him to the flat stone

2

of sacrifice. And I give myself to Him. I, who never speak, who never lie with a man, on this, the Long Night, the longest night of all, I give myself to the God. In a human way. In a physical way. And there is only joy, and sometimes, surprisingly, laughter, and love to be found in it.

***

The God kisses me on the forehead and speaks words I do not know, but yet I feel the meaning. The meaning is love, and happiness, and all the good things of the world. He lifts a piece of my hair to his mouth and kisses it. It is dark against his hand and his face, though his skin is not pale like mine. He has more colour than me, more colour than anyone I know. I notice these things now, in this warm time after love, in the last of the winter sunlight.

He smiles into my eyes again, such a human smile, though without the doubts and thoughts hidden behind it that are usually to be discerned in the smiles of men. And women. His smile has the openness of a child's. It is keen and fast and fearless. Though I never smiled like that when small. I rarely do now. But the God? He is honesty. And truth. And soft kisses on my mouth that summon a smile to my own face now. Oh yes, I smile, today, at the end of the day, at the start of this night.

He leaves as the sun sinks lower; he melts backwards into the trees and vanishes into the snowy silence of the forest.

I know what has to be done, but I resist. For the first time in all the times of preparation here, I don't want to accept others into the Circle, this great and mighty ring of stones. Built long ago by the Old Ones, the ones who came before the Stone People, it is now mine to care for and to keep alive. And tonight I want the place, the stones, the Circle, to be just mine. Mine and the God's. For though he is gone, I know he will always be with me now. There is no taking away what has been done.

I walk the Circle. I walk the stones. Inside and out. In the way of the sun. In the way of the moon. And then the other way, the way feared by some, the dark way.

I do not sing as I usually do in this place when there is no one to hear, as I always do in preparation for ceremony, big or small. For today, all singing has been done. And there was one to hear it.

I touch each stone, loving them, appreciating the distinct shape and form of each. The tall and the massive, the shaped and the fallen, the one with a crescent missing from the top, the one with a deep line down its side. I stop at the flat one, the one that fell long ago into this position where it was meant to be, where it wanted to be. Nobody moved it. Nobody forced it back up. And no one ever shall. It is our stone of sacrifice, of offering, and marks of that are left there this night. Marks of me. Marks of the God. The white handprint in the snow is his, the stain of blood, mine. They are mixed here in this place, as they have been for all time, all human time. I look at the colours until the light fades too much to see them.

And finally, when the sun can be argued with no more, and even the stark silhouettes of stone start to blend into the sky, I walk the path between trees down to the dwellings. Soon the moon will rise and replace the sun in the sky. This year it is to be full on this Long Night. That is rare. So rare, I have never known it before. It is, indeed, a blessed night.

It is time for the men to light the great fire that will give warmth to tonight's proceedings. The God and I did not need it. We had our own warmth, our own heat. My face warms again as I remember, as I bring the memory to the very front of my mind where it blocks all else.

Not quite all else.

I sense other thoughts that are similar to mine. Other people's thoughts invade my mind as they so often do. Many are excited to make their own memories tonight. To lie on the earth with each other. To sing and to laugh and to love. This feeling is all over the place in the air like bubbles in a cooking pot. A pot about to boil over, unable to contain the excitement within.

But now I feel hungry. And cold. I feel the earthly anticipation for what special food Onnagh will have left for me in our home. She will run up here tonight, eyes bright with the joys of women and men. She always does. And I understand this better now. My meeting with the God has enriched my physicality, rather than my spirituality as I might have thought would be the case if told of such an event in a story or song.

I am changed.

And it is good.

The rest of the night will be the same as it has always been. I will sit alone. Eat alone. And breathe my slow way into the dawn.

So I return. To my home. Stane Hame. The place of the stones. And the Stone People. So called because of our use of the Circle, of the stones. Other rings of stone lie abandoned and neglected now. But not ours.

"Morragh is back! Morragh is back!"

In moments their cries change from excited and happy to something that means this night is changed too, along with me, and I am not to sit and breathe into the calm of the dawn. They are removing any calm that was here as they all talk at once, these people, my people, the ones that I love. Busy, buzzing round me like bees, but more closely resembling a terrified swarm disturbed, than happy furry honey makers.

"Morragh, what has happened?" asks Alaron, till tonight the most pleasing to look at man I had ever seen, with his kind eyes and golden mane of hair and tall muscled body.

And then Onnagh, my dear Onnagh: she screams. And it is in horror at the sight of me. It is my name shouted in horror. And the word no. Again and again.

I don't want this. I want to see the special golden smile that my sister usually has for me. I want her to be happy for the Long Night as she always is. Instead, I sense dread in her, a dread long held, in secret, and now manifested. Something she has feared, something about me, has happened.

It is not to be borne. Or understood. And so I flee. To the trees.

It is quiet here, in this high, high oak, with its trunk as wide as a house and its solid naked branches lit by the golden moon. The orb is huge tonight and so bright. It is almost like daylight here in the deep of the wood. I am sheltered, and hidden, though there is still no calm. No quiet. My heart beats fast and loud.

An owl lands beside me and turns her head a long way round to stare into my eyes with her eyes. She sees nothing wrong with me. No need for screaming or horror or noise. She spots a movement on the ground below and leaves, swiftly, swooping down upon her meal, and then she too, like me, and like the God before us, vanishes into the trees.

**

The morning is pink when I return from the forest to our home, our wee house by the pool. The pool is pink too, the water playing with the two different lights from above. The sky is pink and the moon shines like polished metal, hanging low over the tops of the trees now. The surface of the water fair glows with the warmth and peace of these colours, even the edges of the pool are framed by sparkly pink snow and spiky golden fronds of frost.

6

After the meeting with the owl, I walked the bear tracks all night, making them my focus, removing all else from my mind. I did not find the Mother Bear. She evaded me, or perhaps she slept soundly in her cave while I chased another bear, another creature. I stop now to properly observe and feel the gentle pink shade of the water. I try to breathe it in, to let it take me. All calm. All calm. But pink is not what I sense in the dwelling beyond the water. There's no calm to be found there at all. But despite what others may be doing in the house, and what they may be saying, I need to sleep now. I need to be warm. I want to be in a cosy, soft bed now.

So I try to sneak in unnoticed. And, immediately, fail.

"Morragh, Morragh! Look at you." Onnagh is crying. Her yellow curls stick out in all directions like an artist's depiction of a sun, crazed in the heat of summer. It is wrong, it is not how she should look, so it is vastly distressing; her suffering causes my knees to bend and then knocks me to the floor. The emotion is purple. It is blue. A pulsating bruise. Part of my mind stands inside my sister, feeling her from the inside out. This means I cannot hear the many fast words she is saying on the outside. She has to be calm to reach me where I am.

I need calm.

I need calm.

I need calm.

She knows this, but makes no effort to move in that direction. She is so much more than she allows herself to be, my dear sister. She used to sing a song to me when we were wee bairns, 'Morragh, small and dark... Onnagh, big and bright...' but she sometimes sang 'big and fat' about herself. I always corrected her words in my mind and feel like singing them out loud now to shock all the people that are here, that should not be here, to quiet them, to make them go. But I do not. They are too shocked already. Too horrified. And for no reason at all that I can see or feel.

Alaron is present. And some of the women. They form a crowd in this tiny hoosie, not something that is ever meant to happen here in our home. Here in the home of Onnagh and Morragh.

I need space.

I need quiet and dark.

I cannot bear to cause my sister further pain by fleeing again, so I crawl across the floor to my bed, and climb under the cover to where everything is warm and muted.

But they do not go, all these people. They stay, and they talk and talk and talk. I try to go inside myself where it is always still and peaceful, but this is not as simple as it once was. It is because of the God. I know it. My encounter with Him has changed me, changed many things that I have not yet realised, I think. Yet trying to think what these things might be brings a different calm. And that wondrous joy again. It's a joy so strong that I believe I can flow it through this house and bring peace. I touch my lips where his touched mine, and I recall the warmth of our time together. His smile. That open honest smile that I loved so much. The thought of it strengthens me enough to emerge into the room that is full of worried chatter.

I smile what I hope is also an open and honest smile, and I hold my hands high. And the people quiet. For a moment.

"You see the blood on her thighs," says Onnagh in a hushed tone to Alaron, as if saying it quietly will mean I don't hear. She knows better than this. Her distress is causing much confusion in her.

They are all staring at me. Alaron especially, studying, frowning. He steps forward. He comes near, continuing to look at me all the time, right at me. And I look right back. I see his shock. I feel my own. I see his eyes straight on for

8

the first time, and it hurts, like looking directly at the sun. They are so brightly blue. With golden flecks. Gold like the moon. Blue like the summer sky. Him and Onnagh, summer creatures both. His eyes are deep pools of concern. And I feel the depth of my change more profoundly.

"Who did this to you, Morragh?" he asks, proffering my stick.

I take the stick and look closely at it, too. This piece of wood, grown out of a tree long ago, is my way to talk to people, to tell them things and say what I see and feel. I still need it. I cannot speak aloud as I did to the God. Not yet. Not here with all these people. Maybe never with all these people. Any of these people. The thought is too big and new, so I leave it alone and sit on the floor with the stick.

I look at the earth of the floor, the stick held in my hand, its shape made for me, helping me know what to say. What does Alaron need to know? I draw the spiral of the sun. Its light will return and grow after this longest of nights. After the morning pinking of the sky, the golden orb will rise. But I know, in my own light of understanding, that they did not carry out the usual Long Night ritual. I also know, in the same flash of light, that they did not need to. For I performed the required sacrifice with the God himself, and it held more power than any Long Night from any year that has been before. They did not need to pour wine on the ground. They did not need to love one another in the vicinity of the Circle.

However, I want to know more about what did go on, and point at the sun while looking at Onnagh in question.

"No, we didn't go to the Circle," she says, nodding, understanding what I mean at once. "We were looking for you, Morragh." She kneels beside me now, closer, less full of that strange dread, less shocked. She takes my hand in hers and speaks. "Can you tell us what happened?"

I point at the sun and I point at myself. And smile again.

She actually knows that I am unharmed. In some part of herself my sister knows, but she is determined to resist that knowledge. "It happened there?" she asks. "Up at the stones? Some man accosted you? Was it someone we know, Morragh? Or was it a stranger? There is talk of many strangers walking the lands near here. Warriors. Was it someone like that?"

I shake my head. How to explain to those who refuse to comprehend? I do not want to draw a depiction of the God. He is too perfect in my mind, too real to be put into scratchings in dust. So I put down the stick, and place both my palms over my heart. I extend my hands outwards to show my happiness, my joy, my completeness.

They choose not to understand. All of them. They bring me tea. They bring me hot water for washing and a fresh garment. It's when an old lady pats my head that I stand and stamp. Because: no! I am not a wee child, a wee bairn. I am not a tiny puppy to be protected. They have treated me as if this is what I am for too long, and that is over now. A change has been wrought and they must see, and change with it also.

Never before have I joined in the ritual of the Long Night. I prepare it for them. I raise the energies. And then I come down here and sit alone, or sometimes, occasionally, with the very old and very young. I draw pictures in the earth. The very old and the very young like that. They join me in the activity.

I never wanted to do more. I never minded or objected. And I never felt affected by the thoughts and opinions of others like this. I was aware of them. And that was fine.

Well, no more. It is time for an end to these misconceptions.

I stamp again and turn, in a slow circle of my own, pointing at all there present, calling on them to see me now for who I truly am.

I am not a child. Nor am I an aged Grandmother.

I am Morragh. And I am woman.

The Sons of Mars

Alaron and Onnagh are outside talking in low voices, thinking that I am still asleep. I sit by the dying embers of the fire in the centre of our wee hoosie, and observe how their sounds drift through the doorway and mingle with the rainbow rays of early morning light. His speech is low and deep, melodious, blue, hers is quick and anxious, sparks of red and orange, a mother bird, chirping and worrying. She worries so much, my sister, too much, and I wish I knew of a way to spare her this. But I cannot. For it is usually me and my ways that cause the concern and, though I am now changed, it is not, I think, in a way that will bring any comfort to Onnagh.

Alaron is telling a tale from his youth. This is good. I hear my sister laugh as he describes the unlikely hugeness of a fish caught by an equally unlikely skinny weak Alaron.

"You must not worry about Morragh so," he says, and in my mind I shout: yes! I agree with this so much. He goes on: "She is the strongest of us all in many ways. She is," he insists, sensing, as I do, Onnagh's disagreement. "She notices things we don't. Often she is the most focused person among us, even at a large gathering."

"Which is why she doesn't see danger," snaps Onnagh. "Her attention stays on the one thing, be it the fire or the sky or some inner secret road none of us can imagine, and she is oblivious to whatever is around her."

"She does understand danger," he counters. "She assesses people for good and bad when she meets them.

You must know this, Onnagh. I saw her do it when I first encountered her, even though she was so young."

"You mean on the day you found us? When you saved us from the bear?"

There's a short pause before he says, "I saw no bear. Are you sure it was real?"

"Oh, it was very real," says Onnagh. "Morragh attached herself to the creature and stayed with it, and I had no choice but to follow. I couldn't leave her. Even if it meant I was to be all eaten up by the hairy monster too!"

"You were all alone, just two wee lassies, when I came upon the pair of you by the great river. No hairy monster. No creature of any sort."

"Why do you doubt me? The bear must have run into the woods on hearing you approach." Onnagh is cross now. I cannot help feel that childlike sense of gladness that her wrath is not directed at me – this time – and that I can sit and quietly listen to the interesting exchange with no fear of reprimand myself.

Alaron speaks again. "You were so young, Onnagh, and the tale is so unlikely."

"Well, it's true."

"So then, what can such a story show but that Morragh knew who to trust, and who was safe? The animal did not eat you. It protected you both and led you straight to me. Isn't that right?"

Onnagh's answer is an annoyed silence. He has bested her in this argument today.

He continues his reminiscences. "You were but babes, starving and wild, the pair of you. She tensed, as you smiled. She looked at all the space around me rather than directly at me and then she relaxed, knowing it was safe. I knew then she was blessed with a unique intelligence; I could tell she was a gifted one, a child with a connection to Spirit and all the wisdom that brings. I knew I had to bring

13

her, and you, back here to old Yannagh who would know what to do. Without such minds we would still be stumbling through this world in great ignorance, Onnagh. We would have neither fire nor chariots, no one would have had the focus to invent them or suggest such change."

"I know you think this about Morragh, Alaron, but—"

"The other tribes respect and envy the spiritual heart we have here. It's why the gathering of High Summer is the success it always is, and why not a member of the Taezali misses it. And she is at the centre of that, like Yannagh before her."

I feel Onnagh's anger flare before she expresses it in words; a red puff of colour emotes through the door, obliterating the other parts of the rainbow light for a moment, and then my sister gives it voice: "The people we came from did not respect her. She was beaten and kicked, made to live with the pigs—" Onnagh's anger is loud. "Until I bent down to pick her up. She wrapped her arms round me so tight." I hear her voice crack, and know that tears are welling in my sister's eyes.

"You saved her, Onnagh. I hope you're proud of that. You adopted a child who was not your real sister, and cared for her as if she was."

This enrages us both, Onnagh and I. Poor Alaron, for I know he did not mean anything dismissive by his words.

Onnagh expresses our one thought on this issue: "She is more my sister than any birth sister could ever be. We are bound to one another by a force far stronger than blood."

"Yes, of course," says Alaron, keen to appease her wrath, and mine, not that he knows of mine. "You are chosen family, sacred sisters. And it is part of the reason that she is safe now. Safe with you. Safe with us, your chosen people. Safe here."

"No! Last night she was not safe!"

I let my mind float away from their conversation and centre myself, instead, on the fire, and all the small places where the red still glows. The water is hot in the pot where it hangs above the fire. I like the sound of the thought: hot in the pot, hot in the pot. I use the hot in the pot water to prepare tea. I do this with great care, in part so as not to disturb the two outside, or alert them to my hearing of their stories, but also because we are approaching a time where great care will be needed in all things.

A man is coming, and the tea will refresh him so that he can speak his message with greater clarity. Onnagh and Alaron are presumably speaking outside to avoid disturbing me. They must be cold out there. They need to be warmed. I also prepare bread and cheese and add all the remaining dried sweet cherries from our small store to the platter.

We all need this sustenance. And we need it now. For the man is here. It is fortuitous that Alaron is also present at the wee house when the stranger arrives. Onnagh would have sent the traveller on to the great house had he come here first, with only us two sisters present. And large panic would then have passed through the people of Stane Hame before the entirety of the message could be heard and understood.

The message concerns the God. My God. I know it. I feel it. Instantly I recall the feel of his face against mine. The strangeness of it. The beardlessness of it, just a tiny hint of one, a grazing glance against my cheek and mouth. They are tender still from this, my cheek and mouth, but it is a pleasing tenderness, one that summons the sensations and emotions of that blessed moment.

It is with some resentment that I let the memory fade and the present come into focus. Though, one concerns the other and out of them both the future is made.

The newly arrived man does not seem to speak of the God, or say any of the words I am expecting to hear. He tells of men marching in these lands, lands of the Taezali and further south, and further west, further everywhere. Strangers making camp. In great number. It is not what I want to hear, but I gaze down into the glowing embers, and let their deep light take me to these strangers.

I see them. Lines and lines of... Gods! Marching, just as the man said. I look closer. I peer through the fire at them, then fly closer, a puff of smoke in the air around them. These are not Gods. They are but men. Men clad differently from how I am used to seeing men clad. Men behaving differently. I go closer. I go right inside their minds to where they are not so different from any of us. They are hungry. They are bored. They are tired. This one worries about his family back home, back home in a hotter place, a dryer place, but still a cruel place. The next one thinks in great detail about another man and his love for him, his thoughts and feelings not unlike my own memories just moments ago.

Then there is one who I can see in great clearness with no effort at all. This one, he is content, despite the blisters, despite the cut of the strap under his chin. He looks about at the hills and the trees and the sky, and then he turns his head and looks straight at me, thinking of the greatest Goddess of all. And though his understanding of this aspect of Spirit is different from mine, one thing is abundantly clear: she is me. He thinks I am Her. Was Her. Last night. On the Long Night.

We look at each other through the heat haze of the dying fire in this house where I am, and through the mist at the foot of the hill where he is.

We see each other.

We smile.

And we know then what we might have known at the moment of our meeting, but were not meant to.

And, indeed, it is not a whole truth.

For we did become vessels for the God and the Goddess. The great Mother and Father of us all. For a short while, in the Circle, on the stone, in the snow, we were them. Aspects thereof, at least.

But we are man. And we are woman. And now we are changed. Now we are more.

***

The messenger speaks of the Sons of Mars. I focus back in on his words, grounding myself in the present moment and present place, before emerging from the house to see the face of this one who has seen them. He is thin and muscly, and sweaty and tired. He smiles at me, this man, whose flesh needs liquid and food. I smile back as I usher him inside to the relative warmth and hand him a cup.

I want to hear more of his tales and his news, but first: Onnagh. I take hold of her arms as she enters the house. I stand in front of her, holding her elbows. I think of looking into her eyes as I did with Alaron last night. But no. That would be too big a change between us, a shock for us both. So I lean my forehead against hers until I feel a softening in her. She relaxes and – I draw back to see if my suspicions are correct – she smiles. Her mouth is curved into that golden, glowing smile that is only for me. And we are alright again.

So we sit round the fire, all four of us. And as I take my fill of cheese and bread, sitting between Onnagh and Alaron, I listen to the messenger talk.

The Sons of Mars come from a place called Rome. They are camped in great number some distance away. Thousands of them. Line upon line of tents and fences have been erected. Weapons, they have in great number.

17

They are fierce and they are ruthless, these lovers of straight lines. They walk in straight lines and they fight in them too. The terror they have wreaked in the warmer lands is well known. Now they send their spies here to see if they should venture further, if they will brave the territory of the Taezali.

I laugh. For I know they will not stay. It is well known that those from warmer climes can never stand the winters of these parts. But then I sadden. For I know they will not stay.

"Morragh?" says Onnagh, turning to study my face. "What is it?" There's a pause as she decides she knows the answer to her own question. "Was it a stranger...? Was it a strangely dressed man who... attacked you in the Circle?"

I smile and shake my head because I was not attacked, and I wish she would stop saying it. I was not taken or defiled or abused. I took, and I gave. I wanted and was wanted and seen for who I truly am. And for whom I embodied in the moment of course, Her too.

"Their scouts will likely have travelled all over," says Alaron. "They will have eyes in the trees and hills, scoping us out, assessing who they will have to fight to claim this place as their own. That is what they do, these Sons of Mars."

They call their God Mars. My God, my Son of Mars, he may indeed have been a travelling soldier sent to see, an explorer of the terrain. I close my eyes to feel the truth of this and know that it is so. It is a perfect task for a man who feels the beauty of the world as he does, who feels it breathe and sigh and wake and sleep.

"The tribes will have to meet," says Alaron, and I am wondering: when we will meet them, the Sons of Mars? What will my dark eyed man go back and say to the marching leaders? He will not say that he met the Goddess. He has a different name for Her, for me, but I

18

cannot hear it. He will not be speaking any of Her names to the others of his kind. He will tell of hills and forests and great bodies of water. He will not speak of our pool. Though I can see that he has seen the watery, shiny glory of it. He was brave to pass so close to a settlement. Clever not to be seen. Until I saw him of course.

And he is mine now, as much as theirs, his fellow soldiers and their leaders. No. More so. Much more so.

I smile.

A Sharpened Knife

Never have I had so much attention directed at me, at least not in this way. People look at me when I lead a ritual but then it does not feel like they truly see me, Morragh. They see the Goddess, through me. It is what they want to see. What they need to see. And that is fine and good. Now, many days after the longest night, many days after my meeting with the man who I thought was a God, as I walk towards the great house, they see something else.

The women smile and offer foodstuffs and shawls and sympathy to me as they tell their children to run and play. The old ladies are sad, and a bit angry about what they believe happened. The men are wary, keeping their distance, worried that their male presence will frighten or horrify my delicate sensibilities after what they also believe has happened.

It is irritating, but I accept the little breads and berries that are offered to me. I am hungry. There is a small temptation, a thought, an idea, somewhere far back in my mind. I know now, that I could speak aloud to these people and put the fear and sadness to rest. I've done it once. I spoke, or sang, to a man, not a God. But these men and women are in a state of fear, and that carries the risk that I would shock them, and my speaking might only serve to further convince them that some terrible event really did befall me. And could I really do it? Would my voice even work, down here, in a place that is not the Circle? Perhaps I need the sacred space to make sound. Perhaps that is how I work.

I walk round the back of the great round house and approach the workshop of Darragh, the smith. His grey head is bent over some metal he is heating, but he looks up and then lays it down as I approach. He holds out his hand when he sees that I carry the long sickled knife.

I noticed its lack of shine this morning; the blade looked dull, and it seemed to really matter, to need remedy. This is odd. Darragh usually sharpens and polishes the blade for me before a moon or sun rite when it needs to be perfectly bright to slice the light in the Circle. But, somehow, it needs to be done today too, for some reason that I cannot see. The vision is blocked by mist and salty sea spray.

Darragh takes the knife and inspects it with his old, wise hands and eyes. He does not shy away or look sorry for me like the others, instead focussing his mind and knowledge on the task in hand, and for this I am grateful.

He runs his fingers around the curve of the blade and nods. "Go get some broth, Morragh. I'll have it ready for you soon."

Broth sounds good. The great round house, the great gathering place of the people of Stane Hame, sleeping place for some of them, looks good too, inviting and friendly. I walk through the main door where two wee bairns are taking goes to grind grain, giggling as they turn the heavy round stone. My presence worries them not a bit, and I bless them for that, for their innocence and their joy. The smoke from the central fire pricks my eyes, but the smell of the broth is pungent with onion and garlic and something else that draws me over to the pot.

It is quiet in here, not buzzing with life and light as it would be during a gathering, or on the day of a rite. Alaron sits on the biggest bench by the fire, dipping bread into broth and talking to Maddagh, the mother figure of our community. It is Maddagh who will have made the soup I can smell, and that is good for she is exceptionally skilled in the preparation of food.

I hear snoring from the upper level of the house, the sleeping ring; someone must have been awake at night for some reason and is in need of rest now. Alaron and Maddagh turn as they see me and I am surrounded by erroneous concern again.

"Ach, wee Morragh, come sit, come sit!" Maddagh is warm and kind. Always kind. At least to me, not quite so much to small children who seek to steal food before it is ready. Her words can be fierce when that happens. "Now, you just relax there, and I'll get you a bowl," she says, then filling it with purple carrots, and the onions, and the green, leafy garlic I smelled earlier. It was dried last spring, and still carries the essence of that season in its leaves. It is not quite right though, the bowl of food. I sit on the bench beside Alaron and look at his large round bowl and the brown mass contained within. That's what smells so good. That's what I need. I point at it.

"That's meat, lass," says Maddagh, frowning.

"It'll do her good," says Alaron. "Fish her some out."

It does do me good. I love the way it feels in my mouth, all solid and salty and dense. It's exactly what I need.

They both watch me eat. The two bairns from the door walk over and join them as if marvelling at a travelling singer or storyteller come with a song of wild adventure. They are right that it is strange, for I have not eaten the flesh of animals since I was a small child, and the baby pig that I slept with was killed. He was the closest thing I had to a sibling then. This was before Onnagh came and lifted me up. The man I was born to took great pleasure in taking the piglet from me, torturing the wee beastie and then forcing me to eat it.

Such behaviour would never happen here with these people, now my people. It would not be tolerated. Our hunters are skilled and make their kills quickly, for food, not for fun, though I know they do take some enjoyment from the thrill of the hunt itself. They have some smaller fierce Gods on their side, old ones from the hills and forests, and they feel their influence, though they do not know it in the moment.

"It is good to see you eat so well," says Alaron. "And to have you visit here with us again, Morragh."

Alaron believes that when I behave more like the others it is a good thing, a sign of my wellbeing. Usually it is not. But today, with the food, and the quiet calm here in the great house, it is. The dim light in here is like a break from the sometimes overpowering brightness of the world, even the snoring from the wooden shelf above is a restful sound.

"Morragh." It is Alaron, as if speaking to wake me. I have been gazing into the fire for a while. "I have a request to make of you," he tells me. "Would you sit with the ancestor stone in the Circle today? See what wisdom they might send us in these times?" His eyes search mine and widen as he realises that I am looking straight back at him again. He is not used to this yet. Neither am I. I smile into the pools of blue, enjoying seeing them properly, though it still hurts, so I look away to answer, to nod. Of course I will sit with the stone. I love sitting with the stone. What joy there is to be found there, what wise counsel for any woes.

But it is not joy that I find today. And it is not because of Alaron. He accompanied me up the path to the Circle, though he has stayed in the woods. This is not his usual practice. Normally I walk the path and enter the ring of stones entirely on my own. But today he is afraid for me. Standing guard. And that is not a good energy to carry into

23

this space. I can feel his love for me too, and try to hone in on that rather than his worried and watchful presence.

I walk the stones just as usual. Touch each one. And then I take the black ancestor stone from its wrapping and sit with it in the centre. I trace the spirals of the perfect ball that seems to have been made to fit my hand. The marks were carved long ago, when people first came to this land and sought connection to the spirits here. It is a map of the deep underground pathways, many of which we have not found or do not use now, and it is the symbol of this place. I let my mind run round and round the paths of stone until it is as if I am running the deep passageways of old, running, seeking and— argh!

The vision comes suddenly and it is full of pain. I am bound at both wrists and ankles, swaying, blown and bashed and bloodied. The pain sears up through my spine, or down, for I am upside down, hung in a place, a place that is familiar, or was familiar in another time, another life. Voices shout and echo. I am soaked with water and poked with sharp sticks and swords. But it's my wrists that hurt me the most. I struggle to be free of the cords that bind. If I could be free of them, I could run and be free of all this, all this pain and torture and risk. For there is more risk on the horizon. I know it, though I cannot see it yet. I strain to find my way through the haze that surrounds me to see what this means, what it foretells, for I am but in a dream.

I see ahead, through a parting in the mist, past layers of trees, large and small, some bare, some bushy. I see a flash of sunlight on metal and hear the clash of swords. I see shields, strange square shields, all lined up together, and then I see, smell and taste the metal of blood. So much blood. Blood everywhere. Blood soaked into the ground, making it red, pooled in places in the grass, glinting in the sun like wee lochs of death. And then the pain in my body

24

intensifies and becomes too much, the terror too real, and I want to exit the dream, to leave and be safe—

I am bathed in light and love and the scent of flowers. It is Onnagh, her hands, her light, her golden halo of hair that I see above me. She is talking to me, beside me, chatting away as I emerge properly from the dream and see that we are in our own wee hoose, and I am in my bed. "You're safe now, sister," she's saying. "I can't believe Alaron took you up to the Circle so soon after all that happened the other night! What was the great oaf thinking? I said some choice words to him, you can be sure!"

I am sure. I know Onnagh's anger well and, like a naughty wee child, I am, again, glad that it was not directed at me this time. Though that is unfair. For what I saw in the Circle was not the fault of Alaron, who is not an oaf, but a great man. And I do have to tell him about it. This is important. He is outside. I know he is.

I sit up fast and wee sparks buzz round my head like tiny angry bees. Too soon. Too quick. But it is a matter that concerns time. It needs to be dealt with in haste. I force myself to rise and pick up the stick. And then I sit on the floor and draw.

Spring Equinox

Onnagh summons the people to watch as I draw, but the pictures make little difference to anyone's thoughts. I show angry people and the harm that comes from the anger, or I try to, depicting spears and chariots and bloodshed in the earth. But they do not see the wrong in it. They see victory and honour and all manner of other human concepts. They even seem excited as the images appear on the ground.

It is exasperating.

I draw characters and scenes from our stories and legends to show that events as large and terrible and as far reaching as these legendary ones are happening here, now, to us. We must take care. Great care. I draw sea people, half fish, half person. That gets their attention. We are fond of fantastical stories at Stane Hame. The stick forms pictures of the ancient Hill Folk hidden away in their hills. Even people such as them will be affected if we go to war. Winged horses. I know not why, I am getting desperate. But we cannot fly away on such beasts. Finally, I scratch a fierce Calgach, a giant, muscled and hairy, brandishing his sword on the earthen floor. We do not have a being like him to defeat all foes and protect us now.

The people around me are enjoying the drawings, but not understanding the message. So I try to summon peace on the ground, but fail, instead only showing it to myself, and feeling it myself, while everyone else loses interest. Trees and sunshine and flowers are dull compared to the earlier pictures, I know.

So what can I do, then, but shine peace from within and hope that, maybe, it will spread out like ripples on the pool, the pool between their houses and ours, between my heart and theirs.

Putting my stick down with a sigh, I walk out of the house and sit by the pool. I watch its stillness and calm and wish these things for us, and for the Sons of Mars too, who I have no doubt, want it as little as the people of Stane Hame. They too, are excited by chariots of war, battles and bloodshed.

Why? I feel like shouting the word out across the water. I think the sound would echo. I have heard that happen when others make loud noise here, seen the tiny quake move through the pool. But I would bring the opposite of peace if anyone heard me shout or speak. And I do not want that. So I just sit. And wish. And ask for divine help. From the Mother. From the Father. They interacted with one another through me and the God, the man, the Son of Mars. They brought love on that long Long Night. Why could they not wreak peace now instead of strife?

The days grow longer. I visit the pool by our house every morning and every evening, and a little more light is reflected in the water each day. Wee floweries peep their heads from beneath the snow in the Circle, so brave and yet so peaceful all at once. Like we can all be. If we were to have that intention. I tuck some of the pink blossoms into Alaron's shirt but know he does not understand the meaning. He likes the flowers though and is happy that I have shown him this attention, and that is good. Happiness is the excited sister of peace.

"We are to go to Cullykhan at the Equinox," he tells me, and we both light up with pink and flowery joy. Cullykhan is one of my favourite places, and one of

Alaron's favourite places too. "The tribes are gathering," he adds.

There is hope in this. I know it just as I know there is risk of failed hope, but somehow I am able to stay unconcerned about it all. I feel the sun grow closer, warming my face more and more each day as we approach the halfway point between long days and short days. It is as if I grow sleepy, and dreamy. I lie on the thickening grass in the centre of the Circle, and let my mind sink in and out of the doorways of sleep. I see the God, the man, who was here. With me. I remember it all, let it play out in my mind as it happened. In truth I would like him to be with me in the same way as before, and for it all to happen again.

Will this happen?

Could this happen?

Maybe. I let my mind dream and my body warm at the memory of his touch, and his face, and all the parts of his body.

I sit up, shocked at myself. Is this what Morragh does now? Within the Circle, the sacred centre of the community, she spends her time fantasising about men, as young girls are wont to do sometimes?

Well, am I not a young girl?

Not really.

But I am not old.

Though I never felt I was truly young.

Not like that. Maybe I am being gifted that feeling now.

Whatever the truth of it, I would like to see the man again. I would like it very much. In fact, the thought that I might never meet with him again, here or anywhere else, is too sad a thought to be allowed space in my head. Never to see those smiling eyes? To look into them with my own? No. There is to be a meeting of the tribes. It will be to discuss a meeting with the strangers. Surely. Yes. That must be it. I have not listened to most of the talk there has been about this, so I do not know the details of the plan. But meetings of peoples and tribes and minds and bodies – I warm again – there will be. And soon, really soon. Until then, I will let myself lie back in the sun and dream.

Finally, the day dawns: the Spring Equinox.

It takes half a day to walk to Cullykhan up on the grassy ground, through forests, over streams and round hills. It takes much less time to walk to Cullykhan under that ground through the sacred tunnels, and this is the way Onnagh and I are to go, walking the deep ancient path on this day of balance, while the others tread the earth above. Alaron promises to meet us at the other end. I know he is uneasy about us two lasses travelling alone, even though this is always the way of it, but everything is different now.

Everything really is different now.

It is only when I think the thought clearly in a worded way that I feel the full reality of it, the actual force of the difference. The change in the world that led to the change in me, has changed the lives of our people too. Big changes. Small changes. The place of Stane Hame even feels different, like it has been rearranged. Usually when it is just Onnagh and I left here, after everyone else has set off on their longer way, I run about looking at everything in the great house and the surrounding wee hoosies. I dance about the empty settlement with no one to interrupt or stare or speak. But now, today, it feels hollow and dim without all the people, without the chatting and cooking and arguing and laughing and walking and running and sitting.

"What is it, Morragh?" my sister asks.

I shake my head. It is nothing I can draw. It is the knowledge that this place will never be what it was before. Not exactly. And though I know such change is the way of the world, there is sadness in it, and a longing to go back and appreciate all that was before it is gone forever. So now I feel uneasy, like Alaron was earlier when they all left.

The chickens are still here. They are the same. I throw some extra scraps down for them, hoping these are not good bits saved for broth. They cannot be. For we will not be here. There is to be a grand feast at Cullykhan tonight! And the air brightens again.

I skip my feet to the beat of the name: Cully-khan, Cully-khan. I will swim and climb and sit and stare out to sea, to sea, to sea... to see. I shall see something today, something unexpected and beautiful. I take Onnagh's hands and dance round and round with her and then run through the great house where Maddagh left us some food. Bread and chicken... delicious, delicious, delicious.

"It's still strange to see you eating meat," observes Onnagh.

I do not want this conversation again, so I dance away outside and up the grassy path to the spring to ask for the blessing of the spirit there. We will be passing near to underground water rivers on our journey and then arriving at sea streams and pools and the great ocean itself, and this spirit of water, this shiny sparkling aspect of Her, knows all the ways of all the waters in the world. She has been with me since the beginning. With me at all the crossing places of my life, all the moments of great import and change.

When Onnagh and I fled the first place we lived, She was there in the torrential rainfall that washed us as we left. The water cleansed away what had been before and hid any noise we might have made in leaving. She was there in the river that led us to Alaron. And – of course! – she was there in crystalline form, as snow, when I met the man I thought was a God. During that meeting that changed me. And she will be with me today, on this day, of all days... I need to see more of this. I must hear this message properly.

I drop to a cross legged position, under the low hanging tree beside the spring, and close my eyes to feel only Her, to hear only Her. I hear the gurgling flow of the water as it hits the stone below. I feel its sparkling purity. All is well. All is, and forever will be, well, well, well. The water flows where we run, all over this earth, our human lives so fleeting, so worried and hurried compared to the rivers and lochs and seas. Water flows along and through natural pathways and crevices, as should we. It goes gently but with great strength, carving roads right though mountains when it wants to. Cullykhan is a place of water, and I have the blessing of the water spirit to travel there and to be the best I can be there, to do all that has to be done, to say all that has to be said.

No.

She cannot have meant that. Not how it sounded in my mind. But I understand. I will be big and brave and tell the truth where it must be told, in whatever way is best.

I also hear a laugh in the sound of the water, a giggle, as I think about the way to Cullykhan, where we will walk, how the path will lead us down to the water. Something awaits me in that place, something that makes Her happy. Happy, but with a warning. Watch your step, Morragh. Don't make a splash. It is a strange message and I don't know what it means. Some things can only be understood as they occur, and I sense that this is the case with this thought, this bubbling chuckle.

I tear a small piece of fabric from the bottom of my dress and tie it to a smaller branch of the tree above to thank the spirit. She needs it not, but it is a mark to me, a sign of my reverence, and a reminder of the blessing received on this day.

"You will have no clothes left if you keep leaving bits of them everywhere."

Onnagh is right, not only in her words, but in her impatience. It is time to go. I touch a tight leaf bud on the tree. New growth. New life. I hold my hands under the flowing water of the spring and wet my face. I cup my hands and drink of the sweet pure liquid too. Then I wet my hands again and walk to Onnagh who sits on the nearby wall. I brush water across her forehead to give her the blessing and protection of the water spirit too. She shakes her head in consternation, not understanding what I do, but a smile lights her pretty face with acceptance that I do it.

And I remember again the night that we left the place we were born. Two wee lassies in the rain. For that's what we were, and I see this now as I have never seen it before. Something about the change in me has led me to a deeper understanding of the past. Onnagh was older than me, bigger, stronger, more able in every way. I never thought of her as wee or small or even a child. But she was. I keep my hands on her face as I recall more. Things I do not want to see or think of. But the thoughts come anyway.

Onnagh shouting. Onnagh keeping me safe. Keeping the man who thought I was his… keeping him away. She did not get to be a child, my dear sister. Not after she saved me. And I am so sad for this. Onnagh should have been carefree and full of joy and fun and had someone to care for her too.

But that's not how it was.

Not how it is, even.

"Morragh," she says now, taking my hands off her face and holding them in her own. "This is a happy day. We're going to Cullykhan." She smiles her shiny Onnagh smile, nodding slightly, inviting me to join her in this joy.

And I do. For it is true. Golden smiles and Cullykhan are our lot today. And it is time to go.

Onnagh is quiet as we walk back through the trees to our hoosie. We both understand the sacred nature of the deep underground place we are about to enter. I go inside the house to collect my sickle knife. It is so shiny and sharp today, cutting the light in our home, slicing it and reflecting it out in wee sparks on the wall. It needs to be sharp. It needs to be shiny. For why I do not know. I run my fingers round the blade, but no clue comes as to its use on this day, on this visit to Cullykhan. So I tuck the knife into the special fold Onnagh sewed into my skirt to hold it, and head back outside to my waiting sister. We proceed to the wooden well-covering which we pull to the side.

Only it is not really a well, this well by our house. It just looks that way for its own protection and the protection of those who venture within and below. It is a doorway to the underneath, to the hidden, and only we two ever pass through it now. Yannagh, who had our house before us, and was in many ways the wise heart of the community, took us down these old carved steps in the rock when we were small girls, newly arrived and living with her. Onnagh chattered on and on then, excited to be admitted to this secret place, until she saw the dark. Until she felt its stillness and depth.

She is silent now, and still unsettled by the blackness all around us. I love it, as I did back then. Now I know each step so well, love each step so well, each one taking us at once deeper into the dark and nearer to the light. I pause as the steps end and the narrow tunnel begins, already sensing the sea air that lies ahead. Cullykhan. Its scent is not yet in the air, but it will be soon. Onnagh touches my shoulder to steady herself, and I take her hand. Together we walk the rocky pathway inside the earth just as we did when we were wee lasses.

33

Our road slopes down, and the water spirit is suddenly all around us, in the air, on the walls at our side. I stop and press both hands to the side of the rock, feeling the cold damp, adjusting to the space.

"Sometimes I think we should just take a torch," says Onnagh, but that would be wrong. There is light born of water and air here, and how could we perceive these aspects if we brought our own brighter firelight?

The light is brighter now anyway. We are almost there. Now. Yes. One more step and I can see the first misty glow of the Chamber.

We are here.

I kneel in the oval room, this womb of the earth, ensconced by it, held safely and lovingly but feeling so much at once, too much. The space is quiet and dim and still, but it is so full! Full of the memories of those who came before, those who made the walls stronger with smooth flat stones, the same people who built the Circle above. It is only women who come here now, but it used to be men too, before, before what I do not know. Before other times of change that I cannot see, cannot look back at. There used to be a different balance. We are divided now in our tasks, our parts. I understand the gradual way of this, all the tiny instances of change that became big over time. We cannot undo them. We cannot go back. Not ever. And nor should we. We can learn from the past, but we must only ever create the new. Water flows ever on. As do we.

And we all change.

And greater change is coming.

To us all.

I stand. I feel brave. And strong. How I have to be today. To stand against my own people. I frown, confused at this idea. It is as if I am come back to my earthly senses too fully, and too soon, to interpret the end and meaning of a dream. But why would I ever be against my own people?

Onnagh is relieved as we step through the round opening and out into the next section of wider tunnel. It is properly light here, the high roof above open to the sky in places. Dangerous holes in the ground above provide us with shafts of light to make our steps safer. We can see our way and we can smell the sea.

Cullykhan.

It is nearing.

Every step a step nearer.

Still I feel strong. I feel tall and big and brave. Like one of the warriors. I touch my hand to the dragon band on my arm, not dissimilar to that of a warrior, except in its carved design. It's more intricate rather than massive and bold like theirs, formed more like my art in the earth. I touch the curved knife through my clothing. Sharp. Bright. Dangerous when it has to be. I shake that thought off; I have never done anything dangerous or harmful with this knife. The sickle is used to cut light, and light alone. Today my head is full of errant notions, and I can understand Onnagh's daily frustration and concerns about myself a little better.

But the thoughts continue on as I feel the smallness of my being in this high passageway through the land, yet also my hugeness and power. I can do what has to be done. I do not have to be only that which people know me to be.

"Alaron's down there," says Onnagh, true relief in her voice, as we approach the end of the tunnel. "I see him."

I see him too. And I run. I run towards him. I run towards the sound of the water, the sea. And then I see what I came here to see. I see the change. My errant thoughts are given physical form.

Alaron stands waiting at the end of the passageway, the great roaring cave of Cullykhan behind him. I see his eyes, the bright blue of them, but right beside, right behind, I see dark eyes, eyes that I know, eyes that I love. My God flies in the air behind Alaron, and he is glad to see me, and as surprised as I am to see him.

The God, Inverted

My God is inverted. Upside down. His eyes see mine as I see his, and we are frozen and still in a long moment of remembrance. Voices echo around us; Alaron and Onnagh see the God too. They discuss him. He is to be questioned by a man who speaks his language, a man who is on his way, hopefully to arrive later today. There is great excitement running through the whole fort of Cullykhan, about the approaching man of language, and about my God.

I have a moment of slowness and stupidity. Why the need for this other man? Who speaks the language of the Gods? Do not I? I bend my body to the side now, trying to match my eyes with his. To better understand. To better see.

Gazing into those dark eyes, full of human emotion and pain, I remind myself that I know the God is actually a man. It is vital that I fully adjust to that truth now, because this is a mortal being in need of help. And I must tell no one that I intend to help him. I have to be secret with it, so secret and so clever, so canny and quick. For a moment I waver, almost falling over at the thought of a task so foreign to my usual state of being.

I have to deceive. To deceive those I love. I straighten up fast, with a gasp, clenching my fists.

"It is all right, Morragh," says Alaron. "He cannot get free. Though we really need to place a guard here."

I know he cannot get free. I can see that. He has been tied by both wrists and ankles and hung up like a dead chicken waiting to be put in the cooking pot. The top rope is looped over a high protruding rock in this sea cave. I wonder how they climbed up there, the captors, the ones who tied him up. I like to climb everywhere round here myself, but I cannot see how it was done. Yet I have to find a way to undo it. I want to kneel, to sit and connect with the earth and the spirits of the place, and to stay near this one, my one, the God, the man, my Son of Mars. But Onnagh and Alaron are keen to cross the gully and head on up into the bright sunshine and to the great fort above.

Normally I would be keen to do this too. Today I just wish I could remain here without causing concern and raising questions. I will walk slowly and think quickly. These are the only things I can do in these next moments. I must notice everything and everyone and find a way to come back here unnoticed myself. I look at him, the beautiful man, as he sways slightly in the wind. He has not stopped looking at me, not for a second. I hope he sees the meaning in my eyes. I hope he knows that I will not leave him to suffer like this for long. For suffer he does. I see the raw flesh at his ankles and wrists. I see the bruising on his face and body.

And I cannot bear it.

But I cannot focus on this, the suffering. It will not help. I cannot show that I am concerned in any way. Not even to the only two other people here, both so dear to me. I would normally show them anything, everything. But today I have to walk away from this scene as if I do not care, as if I have no interest in the matter at all.

And so I do.

And I don't let myself look back.

We go down the steep incline, up the hill, and down the next slope to the stream. I touch the water, to connect with the gentle spirit again, and then follow Onnagh and Alaron up the steep cliffside path to the top.

The energy on the high flat promontory is buzzing today, so much bustle and fuss of people everywhere. They are distracted and excited, and for my purpose this is good. They pay barely any attention to me at all. It is Alaron they want to speak to, Alaron with whom they want to discuss matters of great import. I keep my face plain, as if nothing is occurring in my mind at all; I am a blank creature with no thoughts. In actuality, I am thinking of my knife, my sharp and shiny sickle, and how it is the way forward for me and the man I thought was a God.

From the high place where I stand, my eyes see the landscape of cliffs and crags and bays, the landscape that usually fills me with such joy and wonder, but I do not really see it today. I am just looking at the soft shapes of land, and the hard shapes of rock, as they drop away into the sea. No in-between places up on top here. No beach, no marsh. Here the space between life and death is painted clear. You could be walking on grass one moment and dead on the rocks the next. This is a place of instant transition from one state to another. Dead. Alive. Happy. Sad. Alone. Surrounded. Hot. Cold. Cullykhan is dramatic, always, but I cannot commune with the elements of it today as I usually do. Sudden death is too real a threat in this place just now for me to contemplate its suggestion in rolling hills and cliffs. But I hope that Onnagh and Alaron will assume this is what I do. The outside of me, the visible part, is behaving no differently from any other time at Cullykhan. At least, that is my intention.

Onnagh soon pulls me by the hand to meet with some other lassies further along the promontory. Feasting has already begun in the small ways it always does before the great meal. I accept a few wee cakes from a young girl who seems pleased that I want them. I take a few more and tie them into a fold of my skirt. I need them. He needs them.

"Onnagh! Morragh!"

The call comes from further along, round the corner of the curved land mass, and I recognise the voice at once. It is Jarredd, our dear friend, who lives here at the fort, but, I know, would like to live with us. Right in our house with us, in fact. Right in Onnagh's bed with her, in fact. He is tall and he is handsome, and I wish Onnagh could see him as I see him. She does not notice the joy he experiences as he sees her, at least not the level of it, as I do. Being beside Jarredd in this moment is like standing near the sun. He burns with a fiery inner flame when he looks at Onnagh.

He asks how the rites of winter were. My sister tells him that they did not take place, and for the tiniest of seconds I see his happiness and relief about this. He is glad that Onnagh did not run up to the stones and partake of the more earthy of that night's usual activities. His cheeks redden, his breath quickens, and his eyes are as bright as his fiery hair. He dampens down all this fire quickly, as he always tries to hide his feelings about Onnagh from Onnagh. It makes no sense to me, even though I am also attempting to deceive Onnagh today.

I hold out my arm to Jarredd to show him that I am wearing the dragon band. He made it, after all. He takes my wrist, turning it one way and then the other as he examines his work and, as ever, a frown forms on his face.

"What is it today, Jarredd?" asks my sister. "Too thin, too fat, too detailed, not detailed enough?"

I laugh. For Onnagh has so accurately described Jarredd's attitude to his craft. He is never satisfied with it. He always wants to make it better. But I love my dragon and have never let him have it back to work on, despite his several requests for this to happen. I hold it to my heart now, to let him know this has not changed.

He grins and says: "It's perfect. Just like both you girls."

40

"Oh, really?" Onnagh teases with a smile, as if in disbelief.

This is where my sister enjoys herself and has fun. Like she didn't do as a child. Here, at Cullykhan, with Jarredd, she is playful and happy. And, play with him she does. Many pieces of beautiful jewellery often adorn Onnagh's arms, ankles, hair and neck, all made by Jarredd. Indeed, she wears something of his almost every day. But never here. She never lets him see that she loves his art. It is a game of sorts, one that I do not understand.

We walk together, the three of us, through the busy mess of people, as Onnagh starts to tell Jarredd the reason why there were no rites of winter. I need to leave soon – I feel desperate to do so – and as we reach the far side of the land that looks over the sandy bay, I see the answer to all my problems.

I slip and slide down the bank, ignoring Onnagh's warning shout about being careful. This is perfect. This is misleading. Here I go down to the beach and sea. I am nowhere near the great cave with its echoes and seabirds and waves, and its prisoner.

Oh no.

They follow me.

Jarredd, I am not concerned about. He is beside Onnagh and so will notice nothing but Onnagh. When he looks at my sister, unlike when he looks at his work, he sees only perfection.

Onnagh is stripping off to swim, a pastime that she loves so much, I think all will be well. She is not a child of the water as I am, but when the sun is out, Onnagh will mix its fire with water, earth, air… pretty much anything really, and be happy.

Aye, there she goes, swimming straight out of the sparkling bay towards open sea, and Jarredd is quick to chase after her. I watch the two of them with great fondness, both childlike in their enjoyment of the day and each other now.

I climb up onto the rocks that circle the base of the Cullykhan promontory and start to make my way round. I glance over the bay and see Onnagh's golden head, her round face pointed my way, so I stop and crouch by a pool as if studying the wee creatures within. It fools her, my poor sister who worries so much, and I watch from the side of my eye as she continues on her way out to the wider ocean, followed by the man who loves her.

I pass by the other caves, large and cavernous as they are. I leap over the gullies that run through the rock and into the sea. No one looks this way. Only wee birds and big birds shriek as I go, telling me to stay away from their nests, away from their babies. I clamber over rough rocks and round to the stony beach, pausing to look up at the high fort above. No one is near the edge, so no one sees me as I run up the dry grassy hill. In my haste I slip and land on my bottom before running up and over the first peak.

I can see him, oh I can see him!

It takes seconds to close the gap between us and draw my knife as I stand on the ledge beside him. His eyes widen. He is not as sure of me as I am of him.

"All is well," I tell him, the words coming as easily as they did before, as if I am a person who speaks often now. "I am here to free you."

Hands first, then he can help. It takes a wee minty to cut through the thick rope they have used to bind his wrists – I have to saw – but as soon as I do, he twists his body upwards and unloops his own feet and is all at once on the ledge beside me.

It is quite a shock to be standing here with him. I had not planned beyond this point. What to do now? I must consider priorities. There's his wounds; they should be bathed and dressed. There's his whole self; he should be moved far away from here and those who might, no, most definitely would, harm him.

He kisses me, full on the mouth, and then we are both laughing here inside the great cave, the sound of our merriment bouncing off the craggy walls of the place. A wave from below splashes over us, soaking and shocking. How this could occur I do not know as it is not stormy, but it makes me stop and realise some things: this man cannot go up the grassy incline for he will be seen, and he cannot go through the cave and out to sea, for he could well be seen there too. Boats will be arriving today. Someone said that, I think Alaron, when I was up on the promontory.

And he could be weakened from his time in captivity, this dear, dear man. I take out the cakes and experience a joy almost as great as Jarredd's earlier, as the God, the man, eats them with such relish and tells me with his words and noises and hand gestures just how good they are.

I marvel at his honest and open smile. It is the same as when I first met him, despite the very different circumstance that we stand in now. He was captured by my people and hung up like an animal to be slaughtered. He is only just free, but not yet fully escaped. Despite this, his full attention is on me, and on the cakes, and then once the cakes are finished, just on me again.

Eye to eye. Me and the dark eyed God.

But he is a man, I remind myself again, a man who can be harmed, and we must go. In truth it may not be long till Onnagh gets worried about where I am and starts looking for me.

And there's only one way we can go. Only one way we won't be seen.

I take my Son of Mars by the hand and lead him backwards into the dark.

A Sister Speaks

This man does not fear the dark as Onnagh does. And I soon realise that he can move quickly through it without guidance. It is not long until we reach the opening to the chamber, the place where men have not entered for an age. I pause and so does he, following my lead. I step forward and so does he. A wave of energy passes through us and blows away into nothing. The rules of the past are gone now. Men will walk this way from this moment on. Finished is the time of women sitting here alone in silence, connecting with the earth. I feel a sadness about this, and a concern, for there is a sense, here in the chamber, that it will be an age before a good balance is restored between men and women, who does what, who goes where. Confusion is all around us.

But we cannot linger. I need to get this man home and out above ground far from here. Taking his hand again, I pull him quickly across the chamber and right along the tunnel as fast as is possible in the dark and up the steps and then, out into our woods.

My heart beats fast as I feel him recognise the place. I watch him looking about, noticing everything with his quick eyes as we approach mine and Onnagh's house.

"Everyone is gone," I tell him, in words. "It is just us here."

I see him looking beyond, towards the great house. He hears the birdsong and the breeze. No human sound. No people.

He turns to me and places his hand on his chest. "Gaius," he says.

"Guy-us," I repeat, trying to say the sounds correctly, and it is the best word I have ever said. Not that I have said many, other than in song in the Circle. But this word is him! It is his name. Guy-us.

He lifts his hand and draws a circle in the air round my face. Me. Morragh.

I have never said my name out loud before. It feels strange as I say it now. It will be strange to him too.

But as he repeats it, that fast keen smile of his forms: "Morragh." He says the rr sound a little wrong, in a gentler way than the people of Stane Hame say it, but it is the effect of his saying my name, not the sound itself, that is most strange to me. I feel warm and like laughing and also like hiding my face from him. In doing so, my eyes are drawn to the rest of him, other than his face. He is entirely unclad, having been tied up that way. So! I have a practical task to distract from the many unsettled feelings that are dancing around inside me.

In moments we are within the great house. I run up the ladder to the sleeping ledge and seek out garments that will fit. Guy-us is slim and not much taller than me, so it is a younger man's trews that I find for him and a shirt that looks the right size.

He pulls them on, still standing near the door of the building as if uncertain whether he should enter.

"No one will come," I tell him, my voice sounding loud and strange and new here in the great house, then leading him over to the central fire and seats. There is bread here and also still some of the chicken from before, and he is easily persuaded to sit and eat with me. His eyes continue to notice everything. It is his work. He is accustomed and trained to do so. But I know he will not tell our secrets. I trust him completely in this.

So he sees it all. I show him the sacred spring. I brush his forehead with the water there, bestowing a small

45

blessing before thanking the water spirit for her earlier message, now fully understood. Guy-us sees Darragh's workshop and the collection of metal things that have been made there. I show him the pigs. The chickens. The old dusty chariot house. And then, again feeling those unsettled feelings but wanting them to settle, I take him back to my own small hoosie in the woods. My name is in among his words then; he knows this is my house, my part of Stane Hame. He sees our central area and Onnagh's sleeping place. And mine. We are beside my bed when I step in front of him, on tiptoe, and kiss him on the mouth.

And then we are on my bed.

And then we are in it.

We are only human this time and it is different. I kiss all the bits of him, all the bits of the man called Guy-us, the wounded and hurt parts too. I will bathe them after, after this time of our love. The names of Morragh and Guy-us sing through the forest this day as we take flight together in spirit, though we also stay bound to the earth.

His eyes on mine. Mine on his. For a long time, this is all there is. Our eyes locked. Our bodies locked. Our bodies moving. Have we become one being? It feels that way for a time, as if we are merged or blended together like threads in cloth to make something bigger.

But we are still moving, moving, moving. Moving in a gentle way, and then a fast way, and then in a way that leads to a storm. A Guy-us storm that spreads out from where we are joined, to my belly and up, to my legs and down to my feet. The sensation is almost too wondrous to be borne and I cry out and cling to Guy-us, clutch at his shoulder, his back, his hair, desperate to hold on to something, someone, him, solid and stable.

I am shaking. He is breathless. We have come through the storm together.

And then we lie, cuddled and quiet and warm. And it is so good. This is how it should be always. This is how it must be for married pairs or groups. Oh. I understand better now. So much. Is this what Guy-us is to me? A husband? He is soon asleep, his breathing deep and slow and even. But I feel in the midst of a storm again, but a mental one this time, and it is far less wondrous. I think of the Long Night, in the Circle and wonder: was that our ceremony of joining? Our marriage? It was sacred, certainly. It was only us there though. And the God of course. And the Goddess. But, no Onnagh. No Alaron. No old ladies to cry or wee bairns to giggle.

But what other ceremony could there ever be for us? He is a Son of Mars. I am a woman of the Taezali. Morragh of Stane Hame. It is too sad to contemplate. So I don't.

We are here together, in my home, and I love that we are here this way. I lay my head on his chest and listen to his heart. It beats as mine does, as all people's do unless something is wrong in them, in double beats. Boom, boom. Boom, boom. Great beats of a drum. I like the smell of his skin, so unique to him. Well not completely unique. I now smell of him too, and this realisation makes me smile.

For a long time I sleep, content and stretchy, until Guy-us wakens me. And it is to tell me he must go, and I do not want him to go. I bathe his wounds with the bitter herbs of deep healing. They sting his wrists and I feel pleased about this for a short unkind moment, because I am cross with him for wanting to leave.

"Morragh," he says, in his unique way of saying it, his head tilted to one side as he looks at me. He touches the angry tears on my cheek, at first with his fingers and then with his lips, kissing them away.

But I am still angry.

And he is still going.

I walk out of the hoosie after him anyway, and he turns and kisses me on the mouth, softly, repeatedly, until I relent, kissing him back less softly, running my hands over his short hair, liking the prickliness of it against my fingers. And then he's going, slowly away from me. Just an arm's length at first. Then his hands slip out of mine and he takes off to the side, towards the trees, in the direction of the Circle. My anger is gone now, replaced with just plain sadness.

"Guy-us!" I call just before he steps into the dark of the forest, and he pauses there at the edge of the trees, looking back. "I love you!" I shout as loudly as I can, causing birds to fly up from the highest tree tops. They make a loud fluttering noise with their wings.

He shouts it back with a wide arm gesture and that wonderful smile of his. "Te-Amo!" I know it is the same message that I gave him and both my heart and my mouth curve into an answering smile, or so it feels, as he melts into the forest, like he did once before. And then he is gone. And I am left with my hand over my mouth, as if to hide my emotions because they all feel giggly and silly and happy and secret somehow.

The forest is quiet and still and changed as I stand there, now alone. Yet I have the strongest sense that I am not alone. I turn my head away from where Guy-us just disappeared to behold Onnagh, now appeared. She is standing beside the well covering, the start of the sacred way. She is so still, she might be a stone. She is so white, she might be a sculpted person made of snow like the wee bairns love to build in winter. But then she is marching toward me, and she is something I do not know. It is not quite anger. It is not quite fear. I think it is shock. And other bad things. She shouts at me, but not in love or joy as did Guy-us.

"You speak?" she yells. "You speak?"

Sword of Truth

Onnagh's anger is different from any manifestation of the red emotion I have encountered before. It is like blood spilled from a thousand women, all at once, and with so much pain. I am knocked down by it, breathless, on my hands and knees, as she barges past me and into the house.

I hear her moving around inside. It sounds as if she is throwing things around our home. I get to my feet and follow her into the hoosie, and then it seems she has just been tidying. A fury of neatening up has occurred. My sister holds my discarded clothes in her arms and is looking at the bed, which is all messed about and disordered from earlier.

She looks at me and speaks so many words, so very fast, that I can hardly take them in. "So this is what you do now, Morragh? This is what you are? You betray your people, you endanger everyone from wee bairns to old women, just so you can lie with a man? A man of Rome. An enemy of us all. Oh, you shake your head at me, sister? But to him, you speak!"

She sits on the bed now, exhausted by her own rage. And the shock. And whatever other complicated things she is feeling that I do not discern or understand. The bed shakes with the state of her. I watch the woven bedding vibrate where it hangs loose at the side.

I have to speak. To my sister. And I don't know if I can. No, I do know if I can, and I can, but it will change everything more than I am ready to have it change.

Will I even be me after it?

Will I still be able to have my silent times to myself, or is silence a way of being that will no longer be mine?

Will I have to speak to everyone at all times, and won't this mean I notice less and understand less and see less of the things that need to be seen?

My relationship with Onnagh. Will it be ruined if I speak? Isn't our communication deeper for the lack of words?

I am panicked and I am frightened. And here, in this moment, surely everything is hard enough without that, without more words, more talk, coming from me to shock and horrify us both. But I look at Onnagh, and I know my silence is causing her more pain than my speaking ever would.

I think this is the case, anyway.

She needs me to speak to her as I spoke to him. Else it is another betrayal as if he is dearer to me than her. And he is not. Of course he is not.

So I must try. She needs to know why and how it happened in the first place. And that it was no slight on her. It was not something I chose or planned.

I look at Onnagh, right in the eyes this time, which is disturbing to us both, so I look away at once. It feels too intimate. Impertinent too, as if I am looking for secret knowledge that is not mine to see.

But I must do the speaking.

And I must do it now.

At first only a croak comes out. It is strange. I find it so easy to speak to the God, Guy-us, I must think of him as Guy-us, not the God, but I am used to thinking of him this way. Maybe that is why it is so easy. I did not know he was a man, a person, a human, when I first spoke. And this is what Onnagh needs to know.

"I thought he was the God." The words blurt out fast, and I glance at my sister to see her reaction, not trusting myself to sense it properly, now I am a speaking person.

She looks as if I've slapped her. Her mouth hangs open in shock. This is what the words did, and I want it to stop. I want to take it back, take it all back, and for us to be Onnagh and Morragh again, how we always were before. Before Guy-us. Before speaking. Before any of this.

I nod at her now, to try and make things normal again.

She nods too and stands up, still holding my clothes. I step towards her and hold her hands around the clothes and shut my eyes and we lean our foreheads together. And breathe. Just breathe. Letting things settle. Letting the echo of the words fade away till they are nothing at all but a dim memory in the distance.

Unfortunately they will never be that for Onnagh. "Wait," she says, pulling back, stepping back, looking closely at me. "Oh, Morragh. You thought..." Now Onnagh thinks, many things and very fast. I can still feel that, still understand that, despite the words I have spoken. And Onnagh speaks more. "You thought this about that man, the man who I saw here today, on the Long Night? You thought he was a God. That's what you mean, isn't it?"

I nod.

"So this is how he came to take advantage of you," she says. "Did he tell you that you had to lie with him?"

"No!" Our eyes meet again as I say this word. It hurts deep down in my belly. Her shock. My voice. All of it. I look away again and choose to speak some more. Slowly now. Carefully. "It was my choice." I take a slow breath. "I led him to the stone." Breathing. Breathing. Telling Onnagh the biggest truth of it all. "And now, I love him."

Her answer is faster this time. And though it contains some of the same words as before, it is gentler. "Oh, Morragh, no."

"Yes."

"No. No, no." Onnagh gets up and walks through into the main living area to stand by the dying fire. There's just a small glow left at the centre now, like her anger, which seems to have faded or burned out too. But she needs her element, the fire, to steady herself and put all the many thoughts in her head into some sort of order. I understand this.

"It is just the feelings of the first time," she says, more calmly now. "They are intense. That is all it is. It shocked you into speaking, and you're still in shock from it. Even speaking is still shocking to you. I can see that, hear that even. I, too… I am not used to it either, sister. But you do not love this man."

It sounds like she's speaking to me, but really she is trying to convince herself that what she says is true. It does not matter. It is her thoughts she is giving voice, and it is good that I hear them.

My voice works much more easily this time. "I love him as Jarredd loves you." There. Two facts told in one go, one small effort of speech. Words, it turns out, are much quicker than sticks and dust.

The flicker in Onnagh's eyes is quicker yet. "Jarredd," she says. "You know we could never… It would be too… This is not about me, Morragh."

I don't understand what she means about Jarredd, but I think our conversation is about her. Her thoughts and feelings matter in this moment, as much as mine. I want to tell Onnagh that I love her too, that she is my dearest person, and no man, not even Guy-us, will ever change that. I want to tell her that I never want us two sisters to be parted. And that I love her. Again. Those are the most

52

important words. But they are hard to say. I don't know why. This most vital of information should have been the first out of my mouth surely. But as it is, Onnagh speaks again and moves the subject away from who loves who and onto unkinder things.

"Morragh," she says with some firmness to let me know it is her turn to tell the truth now. "These men of Rome, Sons of Mars, whatever they call themselves, they are here to enslave us. All of us. All of our people. They are here to change our way of life, to destroy the old ways. It is what they have done all over. For a long time we have believed they would not come this far north, that the lands of the Taezali were to remain safe from their brutality. That we were too far, too cold, too wild and distant to them. Well, no more. They are here. And we are to fight them."

Oh no. It is unfortunate that Onnagh wields the sword of truth as effectively as I do, and I feel the factual nature of what she says. I can smell the blood and hear the clash of metal and bone, but I am unwilling to stand in this particular truth. Surely we don't have to fight. Could agreement not be made? Understanding and peace could come through words? Words can be useful. They can be clarifying. And they must be put to use this way for the good of us all.

Onnagh speaks on: "And this one that you say you love? He is their spy, Morragh." She pales and turns toward me more fully, standing in a beam of sunlight from the doorway, all lit up and golden, as her earlier wrath returns. "What did you show him? He was clad in our clothing." She steps towards me. "You will have fed him, tended his wounds. Oh, he had a right good old time here, didn't he?"

"He will tell none of it!" In defence of Guy-us, speech flows without thinking or trying. I step towards Onnagh.

53

We are now eye to eye, but I do not look away. "He is their slave too." As I say it, I know it. He is, or was, a slave. He is promoted to his current role but still feels possessed as he did in the past. He is not free. But out on the hills and in the forests as he explores, he is free then, and also… "He is free with me."

For a moment the feeling of Onnagh softens and then it becomes jumbled and confused like she's happy and sad and angry all at once.

She sinks to the floor, kneeling, and lays my clothes down in her lap, having been clutching them to her chest all this time, almost cradling them. Now she covers her face with her hands. "It shouldn't be like this," she says, actually crying now. "It shouldn't, Morragh. These events that have happened. I need a moment to think about them, to fully take them in. These two things. You're speaking. You are speaking."

She pauses and looks at me, as if waiting for more proof of that, but I give none. I think my voice is exhausted.

"And you've found someone to love," she continues. "Which should be a happy thing. Both happy things. One is. I love to hear your voice. It sounds as I always thought it would. But the rest is so wrong! Couldn't one of our own men have been enough for you?"

I stare at her. It's what she is saying that is all wrong, all twisted and strange. "What is, is," I tell her slowly. Words are strange. Their speed makes a difference. "There can be no changing it."

Onnagh's emotional state changes quickly after I speak. I see her exasperation. I feel it too. I am finding it hard to cope with what is happening between us – in truth, I want to run off into the trees to have a break from it – but I know that my sister is finding it difficult too. She runs back to anger and hides there.

"Well, 'what is' will have to wait, Morragh," she says, getting up off the floor. "We have been gone from Cullykhan too long, far too long. We have to go back at once. The big meeting is this afternoon and look how high the sun is." She throws my clothes at me and almost shouts her next words. "Get dressed."

I return to my room in silence and dress, obedient in this one thing, secreting the curved knife in my clothing again, for though I now know why it was needed on this day, it might be needed again. And then I pick up the ancient stone ball of the ancestors that has not left this place other than to be in the Circle for time unknown. It gets the sun in my window, that wonderful little doorway in the wall built by Alaron especially for me.

I needed the light.

The stone needs the light.

It feels the rain and the mist and the snow. At certain times I bury it within the Circle itself and it becomes one with the earth. And today, I know not why, but the ancestors' ancient stone is coming with us to Cullykhan.

I let Onnagh boss me about and command that I follow her back to the well cover. She has a need to feel in control again. I understand that and will go back with her, back to Cullykhan. I have no objection to being there, indeed I love it there.

"Are you listening to me, Morragh?"

I nod. I am listening now though I wasn't before, not properly.

She goes on with her instructions. "We tell no one we came back here. We tell no one about the man of Rome. We know nothing about where he has gone. They will surely have discovered him missing by now. We will have to sneak out of the passage and through the cave unseen somehow. But you've sneaked off, unseen, already today haven't you?"

I shake my head. I didn't succeed. She saw me. She knew.

Even when we are on our way and right into the deep dark of the tunnel, Onnagh cannot stay quiet. Thoughts keep occurring to her and popping straight out of her mouth. I don't think it is I that she should worry about revealing something that should be kept quiet today.

"Are you going to talk aloud to the others?" she asks. "Alaron? Maddagh? Jarredd?"

I do not answer. This is not something I have given any thought yet, except with Alaron. I did wonder about speaking to him. But I do not need to answer, as she leaves no space in speech for me to do so. Onnagh's thoughts echo about this ancient passageway as she makes no attempt to be reverent or recognise the sacredness of the space.

"I mean," she says, "they would be happy to hear you, overjoyed even, but maybe this day is not the day to draw extra attention our way. And if you do speak, no mention of the man—"

"Guy-us." I like saying his name. It is enlarged in the small space. And it is different to any name I have heard before. As he is different to any man, any person, I have met before.

We've reached the chamber and can see one another in the dimmest of light now. Onnagh is crying again, her round face wet with tears. I try to wipe them away with my fingers.

"Your speech is wonderful, Morragh," she says, taking hold of my shoulders and looking into my face. "Your eyes too, looking right at me. And your words, you are so fluent, with them all at once. It is a blessing, such a blessing on us."

I am not sure it is a blessing. On her. Or me. Or anyone. But I can explain why I'm fluent. "I always sang in the Circle."

She nods, thinking again. "I think you sang when you were very tiny too. But I'm not sure. Memories before Stane Hame are cloudy."

It's my turn to nod. It is the same for me. With the memories. Some things are not meant to be dwelt on.

"But that it should happen this way," she says, more in amazement than anger, now I think, in this moment at least. "With that man, the man they caught. Of all of them, it was him."

"I took him through here," I tell her, feeling the need to share this information with someone who will understand the deep import of it. I state it slowly to make it clear. "A man passed through the chamber this day."

"He passed through more than that, Morragh," she says, stern again, judging again, and so missing the gravitas of my words. "But I can't think about all this now. We have to go back and behave like nothing has happened. We went for a walk before the meal, is all. We're excited for the arrival of the Calgach."

"The Calgach?" I like the sound of these words in the chamber too.

"Yes, Morragh, the Calgach. He is called to answer the threat to his people. We've been talking about this for months!"

"The Calgach is real?" Surely not. He is a giant of myth and legend, a hero of stories, maybe about someone who lived long ago, of course. Sometimes tales have those seeds of truth in them. The Calgach is a being in a fireside story told to us by Yannagh, or a drawing made on the floor by me when I was silent, but not a living breathing person upon this earth. I find that hard to believe.

"He is the leader of the Caledones," says Onnagh, sounding exasperated again, and then presenting each statement as a question of my knowing it: "The Caledones? A far bigger tribe than the Taezali? In times of strife and peril, the Calgach is the leader of us all? Granted it's not happened in our lifetime, but you really need to pay more attention to worldly matters, Morragh. Then perhaps you wouldn't get into so much trouble!"

As we begin our descent down towards the sea and the, now empty, cave I realise: huge worldly matters are happening here. Now. Not in some fireside story. In our lifetime. Into our lives is come: peril, the Calgach, the Sons of Mars.

A time of great strife is, indeed, upon us.

The Calgach

The cave is truly empty. It feels undisturbed by people, the sound of seabirds loud as we arrive in the opening of the tunnel and stand in the light. It is dimmer than it was earlier in the day. The air is damp now. The ropes that were used to bind Guy-us hang limply from the rock where they're still tied, no breeze to move them.

I follow Onnagh down the gully and up the hill, and then stare out to sea as far as I can see, which is not far. A thick mist has come down upon Cullykhan, making views short and the atmosphere grey and cold.

"The feast has begun," notes Onnagh, looking up at the promontory where no people are visible, but the sound of many voices talking all at once floats back to us. They are within the fort in the main large chamber; I can hear the distinctive wooden echo of the room, and it grows louder and louder as we clamber up the side of the cliff.

Once we reach the fort itself, I touch my hand to the ancient oak tree that serves as a massive door post in this place, and know at once that the absence of Guy-us has not yet been discovered. I can feel the happy celebration of the people within, the anticipation of fun to be had. There is no worry about where their escaped prisoner has gone, no concern at all. I am angered. How long had they knowingly left him with no food and no water? How much longer had they intended to do so?

"Onnagh! Morragh!" booms Alaron as he comes to meet us at the door. "Where have you been?"

I look him straight in the eye, feeling cross with him, but then I soften, because it is none of his doing. I know

Guy-us was captured and bound long before any of us arrived this morning. And now he is free. I smile my joy about this to Alaron who smiles back.

"You are always so happy to be here, little Morragh," he says. "Sometimes I wonder if I would have been better giving you girls to Alara to care for here at Cullykhan, but I grew too fond of you both, and had to keep you with us among the stones."

I shake my head as Alaron leads us to a table and we sit on the bench. He was right to put us with Yannagh; Stane Hame was and is our place. I see Alara now, fair and tall and beautiful, the sister of Alaron and leader of the Taezali along with him, at the head of the long table. She is a good person, a strong person, like her brother, but unlike him, she has no fondness for me. My ways make her uncomfortable and she avoids me if she can. And I don't think my speaking to her would change this. Not that I want to speak to her. Or anyone else in this moment.

Alara is talking to a man I do not know. The man is dark haired like Guy-us, the thought of which makes my heart warm. This man is bigger though, much taller and wider, with a thick beard and a long head of hair braided at the back. The room is hot with so many bodies squashed inside; the strange man is stripped down to a leather garment with no sleeves. On his thick muscled upper arm, cut into the skin with charcoal, is a spiral very like the spiral on our ancient stone ball. I trace my fingers round that design now, hidden as it is, on my person, on the ball, under the table. There is only one person this man can be, surely. I put my hand on Alaron's arm and point at the man.

Alaron nods. "The Calgach," he says with great enthusiasm. "But you girls stay over here where you can have peace and get your fill of food. It is some feast that has been laid before us today." And he heads over to join Alara and the Calgach.

Jarredd soon joins us at our table. "Can you imagine how large an armband would have to be to fit the arm of the Calgach?" he muses.

Onnagh laughs. "But how could it ever be good enough?"

As Jarredd describes the ornate and massive item he intends to make for the large man, I focus my attention onto the food before us. I am hungry.

I can do two things at once, though. I taste each of the different meats and watch the Calgach. I take bites of my favourite bread, the one made with hazelnut paste, as I observe each of the man's expressions. He has a carefully practiced 'earnestly listening' face, which he uses on just about everyone who speaks to him. I want to speak to him, really want to speak to him, and have him actually listen in earnest when I encourage him to make peace with the men of Rome, the Sons of Mars. They are human like us. And they will not stay here, whatever happens. This I know, but I do not want to think about. I let the mist from outside pull in front of that fact, for it is too much to contemplate at this time.

Alaron is speaking to the Calgach now. They seem in agreement about something, expressions true and not practiced. Or perhaps they are just in merriment together. Aye, that is it. The speaking of great matters between them is yet to come. All must be fed and watered first. All must feel as much comfort and wellbeing as possible before huge things are asked of them.

The time of huge things arrives soon enough. Everyone shifts to face in the same direction as if to view a sacred rising or setting of the sun under the sky, but it is to look at Alaron and Alara and the Calgach under the high wooden roof of the fort. I expect Alaron to speak first. I am used to him leading our meetings. If not him, Alara, here in her home. But no. It is the Calgach who stands and raises his arms for quiet. Which he gets. Immediately. There's not a clink of a cup or the scrape of a knife. No sneeze, no cough, no sigh. We all go still. To listen. In earnest.

"Taezali!" he begins, and people clap and bang their eating tools on tables, quiet no more. "I am honoured to sit among such noble and brave people today here in the great fort of Cullykhan!"

The mist comes down around me again. The Calgach is not speaking of the great matters. Not yet. He is chatting, rousing, putting people in the mood for what is to come. He wants them to love him and follow him in whatever he suggests. He will then state what is to be and they will cheer.

I watch him and blur out his words, so as not to be hypnotised like the others. I need to know this man's heart first before I approach him. And approach, him I must. I can see and feel that he possesses true power. It is not like my power. His is an earthly force given by people. Though he has earned it. I feel that too. He has been through much in his life, and he is strong and brave and honest. He is, in fact, well-endowed with the qualities he now attributes to the Taezali in speech. He is pleasing them, flattering them.

And soon he will ask them to die.

And they will do it for him.

Already he has started, talking of the invaders, calling them butchers and rapers. I stop and listen. There is truth in his words, but it is not a whole truth.

I feel the light around me, shining bright through the mist, and I stand, the sickle knife and the stone ball of our people in my hands, hidden no more. There will be but one chance to change the sad destiny of many in this room, and this is it.

This.

Now.

Tonight.

Me. Morragh. Who must speak.

Him. The Calgach. Who must listen.

The room falls silent again as I walk forward, ball and knife held aloft in front. Onnagh makes a small movement as if to stop me but then she stops herself. She knows there is more here than her silent sister in this moment. I am shadowed by the Goddess for this task. It is not to be mine alone.

The walk feels slow, like time has shifted, and I am walking in a beam of light from long ago and from now and from all the times to come. What happens here tonight goes forward and back, affecting all.

Then, now, I am before the Calgach and we look into one another's eyes. It does not hurt too much, this looking, this time. He does not question me or try to interrupt what I am doing. I lay the knife in front of him, still looking into his eyes, and then the stone ball which makes a large hollow echoing sound as it connects with the table, silver sickle encircling it.

The Calgach takes hold of the knife by its handle and lifts it, tracing round the new sharpness of the blade with his fingertips. Light sparks from the metal and flies round the room, touching eyes and hearts as it goes. He lays the sickle blade down and we look at each other again. His dark eyes hold a question as his hand hovers over the stone ball. I nod. He needs to touch it, to hold it and connect with its wisdom.

He takes a fast breath as he lifts the ancient stone, sensing its power. He is a true Calgach, this one, his gifts many and varied.

"Calgach," I say, and my voice is not my own. It is bigger than mine. Croaky and deep. But it causes much consternation in the room. People shift on the seats and exclaim.

The Calgach is not shocked, but he puts the stone down as if he does not want to hold it any more. "Morragh," he says, and his deep voice is only his own. "Who else could you be? I have heard tell of the wondrous summer rites of your people, and you are at the very centre of them. Keeping the ancient traditions alive and honouring the new."

He is flattering me now as he did the whole room earlier. It is a distraction. I ignore it.

"You hold the power of life in your hands, Calgach," I tell him. "And that of death."

He knows. Immediately he knows what it is I will ask of him, and his answer is fast and absolute and unchangeable. "More will die if we do not fight."

And it is over. I have a brief moment of fear, true fear, from those words, his words. More will die. Could Onnagh die? Could I? Might we be parted by this coming fight? But then, the terrible thought passes and I am falling, falling through light and mist. I am wondering if this was why I had to start speaking. To be able to do this tonight. But, I have failed surely? And so fast. And then the mist thickens, and I am falling to the earth, and into many hands that catch me and carry me away to quiet and stillness and safety.

A Discovery

It is dim, but I know where I am at once. I am in Alara's sleeping chamber at Cullykhan, and I know that Onnagh is near. We have not been parted. We will never be parted. Such a thing is unthinkable. I reach out my hand, and it connects with my sister's arm. She is sitting right beside me on the soft bed, and takes my hand at once. I hold on tightly.

"Are you awake now, Morragh?" she asks in a whisper. "Properly awake?'

I am properly awake. I sit up in the luxurious red coloured covers of Alara's chamber, aware of the deep floral scent that that lady likes to adorn herself with. I am also fully aware of the presence of a great many people here at the fort, though they are not here in this room. And for that, I am glad. I can feel their joy and their excitement, though it is, taking the long term view, misguided.

"Alara has examined you," Onnagh tells me. She pauses, and I can tell that she is full of doubt, full of worry. "She says there is a child in your belly, sister. A three month child."

I place my hands over my tummy and know at once that it is true. It is strange that I did not realise this myself, but then it was never a possibility I had ever had cause to consider before now. This was a type of knowledge to notice about other women, not myself. Not Morragh. But Alara knew. More comfortable with me when I was asleep, her examination was thorough and true. And of course it is a three month child. The Long Night to the Equinox. That is the time that has passed.

So new. The child is so new. And so very sweet. I can feel that sweetness as I move my hands over the place where she resides. My daughter. She will do what has to be done in her lifetime, which will be short. So very short, but also long, for something strange and new and unknown lies ahead— I stop myself. I never tell any of the information I glean about children's lifespans to new mothers. It does not serve them to know such things ahead of time, and though this particular knowledge may serve me one day, this is not that day.

"We have told no one yet," Onnagh whispers. "Only Alara and Alaron know."

I nod. This is good. No one else needs to know this. Well, maybe one person, but he is not here. Well, part of him is. My belly warms. My heart aches in a full and pulsing sort of way as I think of him, and how he has left his mark on me. His child in me.

"They have not yet discovered..." Onnagh trails off.

I feel defiant, and protective, and cross. "That Guy-us is gone?'

"Morragh, shh!" Her face moves from worry and scolding to sudden mirth, and she giggles. "I have just told you to shh. When has that ever happened before?" she says and giggles some more at the strangeness of it, covering her mouth in an effort to be quiet which only serves to make it all the funnier.

I make no such effort with my own laugh. It is bold and loud and joyous. "Guy-us is free! The father of my child is running free through the forest, and I am glad!"

Onnagh sobers at my words, and takes me by both arms. "Morragh, it is vital that you do not say such things, especially so loudly, and especially not here at this time. Everyone is agog at the fact you are speaking and will listen to every utterance you make with great interest from now on. You must appear as surprised as all of them when news of your pregnancy becomes known... AND you must be prepared to be asked what you can sense about it – they will all want to know – and then, with absolutely no mention of Guy-us, you must present a falsehood." She looks stunned by her own words as she says them, as she asks this of me.

There is no falsehood being presented by Alaron's face as he steps through the curtain holding a cup and a plate. He is looking closely at me and Onnagh, trying to absorb what he has just heard – and he has heard much – and is now trying to make the words make sense. I can see it is not easy.

He sits on the bed, silently, looking at me in wonder. Onnagh, beside him, stays silent also, but I know she is full of fright. I feel the tiny quiver of it through the bed. The sense of her and me standing against all the others is in both of us again, as it was when we were small, and as it may have to be again now.

Alaron is assessing something. My words, and Onnagh's words, have informed him of some things, but also raised questions, many questions, and he does not want to bombard me with them all at once. Finally he says: "Guy-us?"

I place my hand over my belly.

He understands this. He heard this. "Guy-us," he says again and it is strange to hear the name from the mouth of Alaron. "This is not a Taezali name. Is he one of the Caledones? Or a man of the lesser tribes? And why is he gone? Should we not all meet him?"

"Some did meet him," I say. "Alara would have, I think." I do not mention that Alaron himself was standing next to Guy-us earlier. It feels like something that should remain unsaid.

"Such a day of revelation." He smiles, suddenly and wide. "Your speech, Morragh! Your beautiful voice! What a thing it is to hear. At first I thought it was Spirit talking through you, to the Calgach, rather than you, yourself. But hearing you again just now… is it new? Was it secret? Did you know?" He turns to Onnagh who is pale and wide eyed and full of more and more horror with every word that is spoken.

"I only found out today," she says, quietly as if she does not want to speak. Words can be dangerous. Yes. But not here, not really, with just us three. Alaron will always be on our side, I am sure of it. At least, I hope this is true. It is unbearable to think of him being any other way.

"I always sang in the Circle," I tell Alaron.

And it is only Alaron that looks delighted at this news. "When you were alone," he says, understanding.

I nod, so happy to be telling someone some of my story, and have them be glad. "I thought Guy-us was the God," I explain.

"And so you spoke to him?"

"Yes. And it was so easy."

There is the sound of feet running and voices and trouble. Our happy moment is over and nothing will ever be the same again. This is it. This is the moment that Onnagh has been anticipating, understanding better than me as she often does with many things. And as this may be the last moment of this kind Alaron and I will ever share, I want to extend it, to stretch it out, so I take hold of his hand. "Stay," I beseech. "Do not go at once."

His brow furrows in confusion, and then, ending the moment, there is a man at the door, a man who contradicts my words directly with his own: "Alaron, you must come at once."

"I will be there shortly," Alaron replies, squeezing my hand, as Onnagh, now standing behind him, looks like she might be about to be sick or fall down.

"The man of Rome is gone," explains the one at the curtain. "He has been cut free and fled."

"No!" says Alaron loudly in shock, now standing, now going. "We should have set a guard. I meant to say to someone, that there should have been a guard, if not a few. But then I got caught up in everything and with everyone."

He's moving. He's going. I don't let him. I grip onto his hand and his arm, so saddened by this loss, what could be the loss of him and his golden light from my life.

"Morragh," he begins, as if to comfort me, and then he stiffens as he works it out. The prisoner is gone. Guy-us is gone. And he knows. Alaron suddenly knows they are one and the same. "No," he says again, soft this time, saddened like me, and full of fear and dread and disbelief. But then he shakes his head free of the truth, choosing in this moment, at the very end of the moment, to misunderstand after all. For now, at least, he is delaying the fullness of knowledge, and all that it means.

"We will speak soon," he says to me, proffering the plate and the cup. "Eat, Morragh, regain your strength."

And, along with the other man, he is gone. So much gone. Too much gone. But the wine is sweet. And the meat is good.

"How can you eat?" demands Onnagh, sitting down on the bed, filling the space that held Alaron just a moment ago. "He knows! Alaron knows. And we must now do the same as your raping man of Rome and flee. You have lost us our home, Morragh."

"You know there was no rape, sister. Oh, Onnagh, the wine is good. It is bramble. Have some. It will calm you."

I hold the cup out to her, but she knocks it from my hand and it splashes everywhere. Red on the red covers. Red on the red walls. Alara likes red. She likes comforts. She will not like the spilled wine though.

It all looks so much like blood. So now this is all I can see. Blood on the bed. Blood to come. Blood on the curtain and the walls. Death to come. Life blood too. For we are not bleeding, Onnagh and me, not dying. For now, we are still very much living. But we are not gone. No one is ever truly gone. Not gone from this place. Not gone from these people, who are still very much our people. And so will they ever be. In one form or another.

"I am going to join the people," I say, standing, steady and strong. "Our people."

Onnagh has wilted like a summer flower after a storm. She watches me, wide eyed again, as I hide the sickle knife and the ancestor stone in my clothing once more.

"They will kill us," she says, her voice barely audible.

Now it is me that is loud and clear. "They will not." The words ring with a note that is only ever heard, felt, experienced with a statement of absolute truth. "No Taezali or Caledone will ever kill us, Onnagh. And I will never present a falsehood to them."

She follows me out of the chamber like a wee lost girl, not believing my words, or rather fearing what they mean, and so trying not to think of any of it. Things were definitely simpler before I started speaking.

Most folks have gone out onto the ramparts, and when we join them, I see many wee lights being carried between the promontory and the sea cave. People are scurrying about like rodents discovered in a grain store, fearing for their lives, wondering where they should run to and waiting for doom to befall them.

"It's Morragh! It's Morragh!" The cry goes out as people part ways so I can walk through them to the cliff edge. I hear their whispers and mutters. "Will she speak again, do ye think? What will she have to say of this?"

The news of my emergence travels the gully fast, and I soon see the tall figure of the Calgach come to stand on the ridge, dark against the light of many lanterns behind him, just in front of the cave where Guy-us was tied earlier.

"Morragh!" shouts the large man, raising his arms in front of him, and I am summoned.

His words hold power, as mine sometimes do, though his have a stronger edge of command. I let myself obey that command now and flow to him, down the hill and over the stream and up the ridge to stand right beside him. The people, who were panicked only moments ago, all come too, following on, steady and calm now. Onnagh is near me. I know that without looking round to see. I have a large gathering of men, women and children at my back, while he – the Calgach – has only a few of his own warrior men beside him.

"The man of Rome has escaped," he says, voice deliberately loud and carrying so all can hear. "His ropes were cut, and there is no sign as to where he has gone. What can you tell us, Morragh? What can you see?"

I smile at his attempt to use me as some sort of elderly soothsayer who stares into the guts of animals to divine half-truths. But I can give him what he wants. I can give our people what they need in this moment too.

It is all so simple.

And yet not.

I have spoken to Guy-us. I have spoken to Onnagh and now Alaron too. But all these people? Together at once? It feels impossible. Too daunting. I am terrified. I see Alara standing beside Onnagh and Alaron, looking over at me with them. She looks displeased. Sceptical? I'm not sure, but her unfriendly stance unsettles me further.

I want to run. To hide somewhere. To be a wee quine again.

But I don't give in to these feelings.

Instead I raise my hands high and close my eyes. And speak, loud and clear as the Calgach did moments ago. "No danger will come from the events of this night."

My voice echoes around the cave and then there is silence. Only the lapping of small waves against rock can be heard. There is no whisper, no breeze, not even the call of a gull. I open my eyes and observe the thick mist that surrounds Cullykhan. It hangs like an impenetrable curtain of protection around the people and the place. And the Calgach. And me.

Warmonger

The mist makes the many small lights of our people grow great, as I turn to behold the Taezali behind me. A huge cloud of golden light surrounds them, but I am standing outside it. I have stepped away to stand in a different light. I turn back to face the Calgach whose gaze, I know, has never left me.

He breaks the silence, as I knew he would. I was waiting for it. As we all were. He smiles and then he laughs, holding a hand out in my direction. "This one, she cuts through the confusion of men and goes straight to the heart of the matter. You say we are safe enough, Morragh?"

I nod.

"On this night we are safe," he agrees, but there is an edge to his words, an angle, a purpose. "However, the ones who rescued our prisoner, they will attack at some point. In the dawn as we sleep, perhaps?"

I shake my head. Indeed, my whole body feels shaky, so I bend my knees and sit on the rock at the top of the ridge, there beside the Calgach, pressing my hands down onto the stone.

I take a breath and raise my head as the clouds above begin to clear a little. The moon shows golden through the mist now, high and bright in the sky, ringed by copper and bronze and dark, dark blue. It is not full tonight, but its colour reminds me of how it looked on the Long Night. How it looked on the night when I first met Guy-us. And this connection lets me see something. "The man of Rome who hung here, upside down in the cave, now stares at the same moon," I say, pointing up, keeping my eyes on the sky. "And he stares alone."

It is true. I can see him, and I can see right through him to what he sees. He is deep in the forest, gazing up through a rounded break in the tall, dark trees around him. I can smell the pine and feel his loving thoughts of me. The gold of the moon has reminded him of that first night, that Long Night, too though it had not risen when we met. It rose later when I was in the forest by Stane Hame. He was among trees then too. The forest floor is soft where he is, and the air damp, though it is not as misty as it is here at Cullykhan. He has moved some way inland.

I must move too. My own small light is not enough to influence the Calgach at this time, though a change has been wrought this day that will allow greater forces to affect him. The change is not just in him, or for him. It is imperative that I change quickly too and become used to speaking. Speaking a lot, and speaking to many. Whenever it is required. And it is required now. And I have to do it just as loud and clear again, so that all will hear. In fact, in time, all may be involved in the matter that I am about to speak of.

I want to waver. I want to let my poor, weak human side win, from the crying little girl I once was, to the pregnant woman who really just wants rest and food and wine and peace and sleep and a quiet simple life with the man she loves.

The Calgach is moving as if to speak, but I know I must do so first. I stand again, trying to be tall, and address him by his title; while he holds it, while he lives, it is his name. My voice is not only my own. She has lent her power to me in this moment which means all the speaking comes easily.

"There is a sacred place known to my people," I say. "A chamber. A womb of the earth." All is silent again.

Lapping waves and held breath. I go on. "For as long a time as is known and understood by us, this place has been the domain of women. Today that has changed."

The Calgach's eyes burn bright with excitement. He likes this drama, this story, and he knows he will have a special part to play in it.

I cut straight to it. "I invite you, Calgach, to walk the ancient passage and step within the chamber to receive the blessing of the Goddess."

There is no thoughtful pause before he answers. His reply is immediate: "I accept."

But I will look for pause now. It is essential that I see in to the heart of this man—

What I get is interruption. For the briefest of moments I am annoyed, but only for the smallest second. For it is Alaron who has put his hand upon my shoulder, and Alaron whose face is full of concern. "Morragh, will I accompany you?"

Knowing what he knows about Guy-us, he still stands here for me, keeping me safe. And I wish, in a way, that it was him I was to take into the chamber. It would be an infinitely more joyous occasion. I put my hand on his cheek and look straight into his eyes, though it still feels like a great impertinence to do this, and then know that this can be, it will be, just not at this moment.

"Later," I say, noting that he is still shocked by my speaking. I lower my voice so only he can hear. "Your blessing will be different. The Calgach is to be tested. You do not need to be."

He nods, squeezes my shoulder and touches my face as if I am still a wee lass somehow, and then he steps back.

I turn back to face the Calgach, but I speak no more. He is to go first. Into the dark. To face it as if alone. And see what comes.

I watch every expression and movement he makes. I see the small twitch of his head when I raise my hand to the side and point to the nearby dark entrance, indicating that he is to enter the passage first. He stands taller at once, brave, up to the challenge, or so he believes. I hope he is right. I do not want to envisage a situation where he is undone. So I stay in the now, right in this time and place with the great tall man that is the Calgach.

He walks through the opening and barely falters as the dark takes us, but he does hesitate ever so slightly. And that is good. It is not wise to walk into this place in any way arrogant or thinking oneself above such feelings as fear or doubt. They are human emotions and we are human. Guy-us, earlier, was full of thankfulness and joy, beloved faces of the Goddess. But his situation was different. And I am not here to compare men. I am to test and bless this one who walks in front of me now, and whose decisions are to affect the lives of many.

The Calgach keeps walking, touching the damp walls in places to steady himself. He must know that I am here, but he does not attempt conversation. Which is good. Because I have none.

The path steepens and becomes rougher, taking us uphill to the chamber. I put my hand on his back and he stills, awaiting instruction. I press him to the side and he obeys, and turns where he is pressed. Then he makes a mistake. He does not pause before stepping into the sacred space. He does not sense the need for this reverence. But it will not be his undoing. He is just not that sort of man. He is the sort of man he needs to be for the life he was born into. And this is not so much a test as a training ground. And it is not me that will provide the training.

Already I feel floaty and light. Some of me is leaving, making way for Her as has happened many times in the past, but never quite like this. Aspects of Spirit that I have never encountered before are with us here in the chamber. Fierce aspects. Shouting. Screaming. These are cries of war and grief, and the voice that rises from deep within my belly is coarse and forbidding.

"Kneel," is the instruction to the Calgach, and he obeys at once.

My feet walk a circle round him and then another and another as his breath quickens. I feel a need to cast some form of protection over him before he faces this challenge. Nay: this ordeal.

"Calgach," the voice continues, and my hand reaches out and grabs his hair then stays there on the top of his head, pulling tight.

"I am here," he replies, brave, oh so brave.

"Warmonger," is the accusation.

"No," he responds.

"Warmonger."

"No, I—"

"You argue with me?" The voice is harsher now, rasping, its roughness hurting my throat. My hands are no longer my own. She is moving them, using them. My beautiful knife, used earlier to free a man, is suddenly brandished high in the air. It catches the small amount of light that there is in the chamber and throws it about the air and walls in small sparks. The Calgach's eyes dart about, following the sparks, his mind trying to make sense of what is happening.

And then the knife is at his throat, the curve perfect for this purpose, the sharpened blade perfect for this purpose. And it draws blood.

Forfeit

I feel the warm blood of the Calgach, wet and sticky on my fingers, as he falls forwards, his hands at his neck.

"Women have always bled to bring men into this world," She says. "Now a man bleeds in my ancient womb. What does he seek to birth?"

Hands still at his throat, he speaks: "Freedom."

"Men mean many things when they speak of freedom."

"Not I." His head is higher now, revealing what is thankfully only a small cut on his neck. He has dropped his hands, though he remains kneeling which is wise. She likes my knife. She turns it round and round in my hands as she speaks.

"I want freedom from the oppression of Rome," he explains. "Freedom for our people."

"Do you ask for my blessing?'

"Aye," he says, head up, looking straight at me now, at Her. "Will you bless me in leading the tribes against the foreign foe?"

"Such a blessing bears a high price. Are you willing to pay it?'

"My life," he says, understanding before I do, agreeing with no hesitation, and continuing on determined: "Will we win against them?"

"Win..." She says, and the word swirls around us. Then, as if She is bored or tired of the encounter here in the chamber, She speaks fast. "You will win the war. The troops from the South will leave this island, and they will leave these northern climes first, in part due to the choices you are to make. But you will not win the battle, Calgach. The Eagle will fly over your lifeless body on that day."

There is a pause. My legs bend in readiness, my arms tense, and then I jump forward wielding the knife. "My blessing is yours," She says, and nicks his throat with the end of the curved blade.

The Calgach and I are alone once more, and we are both left in shock. I reach out to check the cut on his neck but he is barely hurt. It is a wee scratch, no more. "For a moment I thought your life was to be taken this night," I say, so glad that this was not the case, then explaining: "She is gone."

"Aye," he says, sinking to sit on the ground. "I ken."

I sit right down too, released, just Morragh again.

"You and I," says the Calgach, softly, not returned to his usual loud self yet. "We are very alike."

I look at him and almost laugh, for it is a truly laughable thing he has said.

"We are," he insists. "We are both leaders of our people, one earthly, one of the spirits and sky. We would make a good match."

I stop myself laughing this time, for it would be to dishonour him. "You do me great honour, Calgach," I tell him, looking at the ground rather than at the man. "But it is not my path."

"Not as a married pair, then," he says, in no way seeming offended or saddened. "But we are linked. And everyone needs to see it. It will strengthen both our positions and, in turn, give strength to the people."

"You need food," I tell him, looking at him now, standing and holding out a hand. "It will bring you back to the earth fully."

He stands slowly, and I can tell from the way he moves that he is still considerably shaken, though he holds himself tall as he looks around.

"My eyes have adjusted," he says. "And I can see this place better. May I touch the walls?"

"Yes." This too, will give him strength.

"Who built it?" he asks, as he feels the smoothness of the stones.

"It is said it was built by the Old Ones. The ones who came before the Stone People. Their Circle is above."

"Aye," he says, nodding, though sounding less certain. "I have heard tell of it."

So I take the hand of this man who has just been told he must die, and we walk the path together back to the people, and the mist, and the golden moon, and the many wee lights.

As soon as we step out into the relative open of the sea cave, and the lights of the people, the Calgach raises our joined hands high for all to see. He is back in his domain. "Today," he declares, booming it out so all can hear, the word echoing round the cave. "Today," he repeats slightly less loudly, "Morragh and I have joined in purpose, and together, all of us, we will rid this land of the invading foe!"

The noise level is unbearable as all the different sounds - shouting, cheering, talking, excitement - rebound off the walls of the cave again and again.

"Food," I remind the Calgach before slipping my hand out of his and slipping myself down into the crowd, closely followed by Alaron who had stayed by the tunnel entrance. Onnagh is there too, and we three climb the cliff back up to the fort.

"Morragh, stop," she says as we reach the top. "Stop and speak to us. Tell us what transpired between you and the Calgach in the chamber."

I really don't want to have to speak again, but these two, so dear to me as they are, and I to them, deserve to hear what has been said and decided. "She blessed him." It comes out as a whisper, for I have little voice left this day. "I don't know what he is to tell everyone; that may have been all he will say about it down there."

It's not enough for Onnagh. "But us, Morragh. You can tell us more?'

"Sister," I say and take her hand, and look up at Alaron, knowing and feeling who he is to me in this moment too, this lifetime. "Father."

He smiles, pleased by the title, I think. "We are alone on the cliff," he says. "What you say here will remain between the three of us."

We are, indeed, alone. There is the sea at one side and the grass underneath us; the nearby rocks and cave are obscured by the dark of night now. My mind is working, trailing along human pathways and deciphering all that I heard in the chamber.

"I do not want either of you anywhere near the battle that is to come. I do not want Guy-us there either." Onnagh squeezes my hand, too hard for comfort, more like a warning not to say too much. What a strange new problem for me to have. But Alaron knows of this, of Guy-us. He has not thought about it yet, not let his mind trail the pathways, but deep down he knows of my betrayal, just as I know: "Guy-us will be there though, whatever I want. That is certain."

"This was said to the Calgach?" Onnagh sounds disbelieving.

I shake my head. "The Calgach was told that his own life is forfeit. He accepted it bravely. Rome will leave, yes. But we will lose the fight on the day of battle." My voice is a wee croak now like the smallest of baby frogs back near the sacred spring at Stane Hame. I feel that aspect of Her near me in this moment, and she is so different to what we encountered within the earth tonight. So much softer and giving. She flows all around us, she is the sea and the mist – of course she is the mist – and she dances all round the baby in my belly too. "I need food," I say.

And then I am dropping and being carried, all the way back into the fort and into bed. Alara's bed again. This is where we are to stay, Onnagh and I. This is strange. Are we being honoured? Or kept an eye on? I don't know and I cannot think on it now. There is a little wine and a little meat and then, just as I am falling away to sleep, I remember something that Onnagh would like to know. It involves a subject that has always very much interested her.

"The Calgach," I whisper to her. "He proposed a match with me."

"What?" she gasps. "A marriage? And what did you say? Morragh! Do not tell me this much and fall straight to sleep. Tell me sister…"

But clouds of comfort have found me, and Onnagh will have to wait.

First Gift

I am stretchy. I am warm. And it is so lovely to hear the voices of Onnagh and Alaron outside. No, not outside. Closer. Right here in this room with me, at Cullykhan. I love that they are so close. My dear Onnagh. And dear Alaron. They are speaking in hushed tones so as not to wake me, and I lie here luxuriating in their caring stances and in the soft comfort of the bed, and the cosiness of the blanket until… their words begin to make sense, and it is horrifying.

"He is not a spy of Rome!" I declare loudly.

"Morragh, shh," urges Alaron. "We do not want to be overheard."

He is right in this of course, but I am still inflamed with rage at what I heard Onnagh saying. I climb out of bed and stand toe to toe with her and hiss: "Guy-us will not tell of anything that he saw at Stane Hame or Cullykhan."

"Oh," she says, hands on hips, furious too. "That's good then, as you showed him absolutely everything!" She tosses her head and her pale hair seems to flow around her face like many angry snakes, all glaring at me together.

"And why should I not show him?" I ask Onnagh and the snakes. "He is my… my…"

"Your what, Morragh?" Her voice is scathing, her words cruel. "He is not your mate, your match, your husband. He can never be that. You were offered the greatest pairing any lass could have yesterday, and I'm guessing you said no?"

Words have left me – in truth I am amazed and a little shocked that they came so swiftly and naturally to me in my rage – and I sit back down on the bed. Because what Onnagh says is true. With the state of things between our peoples, Guy-us can never be my husband, never be accepted by the Taezali or into our home. He will never be beckoned towards the fire to have food made by Maddagh, never have his knife sharped by Darragh.

"Ah, now, come." Alaron sits by me on the bed and I lean against him as the sadness flows. His arms come round me. "You did not know who he was," he says. "You are without blame there, Morragh. But it is best that the identity of your baby's father is known only to us three. For everyone's safety."

This is true. The Taezali strung Guy-us up just for being a Son of Mars, just for getting caught. They would do far worse if they knew this about me. The story of rape would abound because of how they all treat me, how they view me. Onnagh keeps repeating it, even though she knows the details now.

"She is not without blame for his escape—" starts Onnagh, but Alaron silences her with a raised hand.

"This we speak of nowhere ever," he says, and I sense that he does not want this fact to solidify even in his own mind; it is not just about keeping it from the others. His next words are simpler: "Now, let's get breakfast!"

The Calgach is already at the long table in the great room and he calls us, well, me, over at once, but we all go. "Will you sit beside me, Morragh?" he asks and I agree.

"This is my sister, Onnagh," I say. I will not have her left out. She should sit at the high table too.

"So, I am to be surrounded by beauty," says the Calgach, his charm and talent for flattery evident again along with his wide smile. But it is not insincere, and I find that my feelings for the man have warmed. He is truly brave and selfless in seeking continued freedom for our people, despite what he was told last night. I know he believed the telling. Some men, lesser men, would have slipped away before dawn, while everyone else was sleeping, to escape the predicted fate. He has not.

I sit between him and Alaron. Onnagh is honoured on the other side of the Calgach and she seems pleased with this, placated for now at least.

Once conversation and eating are well underway, the Calgach leans toward me and says: "I urge you to reconsider the proposal I put forward last night, Morragh. The wife of a Calgach will be revered and cherished by all the peoples for as long as she lives. You already have your own high status, and would add this to mine, making our leadership stronger. Our match would give you increased protection, even when I am gone, and I very much like the idea of that."

He speaks of his own impending death with no resentment, no fear even, though I seek the shadows of these feelings in his warm brown eyes. I can give him only honesty in return.

"'I am not what you think, Calgach. I am with child."

"The child would be protected too," he says with not a blink of judgement or surprise, none of the usual preconceptions of me as innocent and pure evident in his voice or face.

"The child has her own special task," I tell him, closing my eyes to see more, but dense mist still hangs in front of this future, the future of my daughter. "It is to do with all that takes place just now, but I am not being shown… It will be revealed in the right time."

The Calgach nods. "Aye, it's not always the best thing to know in advance."

I reach out and squeeze his large hand. He is right. It is not. He and I were treated roughly yesterday. Especially him. He turns his hand so he can hold mine.

"It will take months for the enemy to amass the warriors they need to fight us," he tells me. "High Summer would be a good time for a gathering of the tribes. What would you feel about Stane Hame and your Circle being the place for it?"

I feel the rightness and power of that and nod.

He goes on. "Could there be a ritual with you and me at the centre? In some way? Would this work?"

"I will have to sit in silence to discover the answer to this."

"And blessings for all, as I was given last night?"

"Yes." I never refuse blessings for anyone. And I can see at once that they are all going to want them. And why should they not? With what they are being asked to do, to risk?

I am numb as I look out over the large space under the high roof. People are gathering to fill their bellies, feed their bodies. Those bodies that are so fragile, so easily harmed. And they are going to be. Harmed. Many of them.

"Eat, Morragh," says the Calgach, releasing my hand and passing his plate of roasted meats over to me. "There is much to enjoy in this life."

It is true. And who knows when any of us will die, after all? We need to appreciate the gifts of the Goddess, and of the earth, while we can.

But, three days later, as we ride back in the sunshine, above ground this time, I feel differently about things again. Specifically about the many blessings. I think of the chamber down in the earth, the place I do not feel quite ready to enter again so soon. It is where I was told of one impending death, and where I will be told such things again. All the Taezali must be offered the chance to visit it for blessing. Not just those of us who live here, the others too, the many, many people who will visit at High Summer. So it won't just be the Taezali. There will be the wider tribes too. All the tribes. I will place my hands on an unthinkable number of heads.

There will be no more tests with the knife, but I will know things I'd rather not know. I will see. But they don't have to, the receivers of the blessings. It was only the Calgach that had to be told. That was a unique event. An unkind event. It will not happen that way again.

I look at the gorse, one or two wee yellow flowers to be seen. I look over at Onnagh. She is finally more relaxed and happy, thinking the worst is over. She thinks only of our deceit; her relief is that we got away with it.

I hold tight to Alaron, my arms wrapped round his strong back, as we ride, and I know that the blessings will not be blessings for me. I am to be cursed with too much knowledge. The thought of it overwhelms. I close my eyes and try not to hear anything either. There's just the movement of the horse beneath me and Alaron's heart near my ear. Life. Warmth. Goodness. I feel the heat of the sunlight on my back, golden and giving, intense in its power. I hear the wind in the trees and know that we are close to home, where I want to be, all curled up in my bed.

I am exhausted from answering the many questions from, oh so many, people about my voice, and how and why I speak now. The truth is that I do not have the answers they seek. I have wished that this change had not happened many times over the last few days, and that I could just sit in silent observation as I usually do.

And everywhere, from almost everyone, there was an implied assumption that I am in some way 'better' now. As if I was broken before and a miraculous healing has occurred. This is nonsense. I am no better than I was before. I was fine then, the way I was. I will have to find a way to be fine now.

I overheard Alara expressing the idea that I could always speak and just chose to do it in public now to help our cause, or perhaps to gain attention from the Calgach. Neither idea is true, of course. She places her own thoughts about how she might feel in similar circumstances onto me, and they do not fit.

One question was different from the rest. Jarred, the sensitive and thoughtful artist, asked: "Does it make you happy, Morragh, speaking like this now?" I could tell he wanted to know this sincerely, that he truly cared about it. But I could not tell him, for I do not know the whole answer. My voice has not, so far, made me happy. But, who knows? Perhaps one day, it will.

I do not speak at all on the ride, and the journey is soon over. And then I make straight for our wee hoosie, but pause before entering. Something is different. Someone has been here in our absence. Something has been put near the door. It is a tiny clay vessel, like a beaker or a cup but with a thin neck leading to a closed top. It is shapely and beautiful. I lift it to my face and know at once from where it has come. I know who left it here for me, and I smile. The Calgach was not wrong. There is to be joy too, in amongst the turmoil, and this wee gift is just the start of it.

Forest Glade

"What is that?" Onnagh's voice is sharp when she catches me examining the bottle, as if I am a naughty little child up to some mischief.

I pull the stopper of the container, and find that it is wound round with the stem of a flower, a tiny pink blossom that I recognise as one that grows in the Circle. It is found in many other places too of course, but I know this one came from the space between the stones.

I tip the vessel carefully and some liquid comes out onto my hand. "It is oil," I tell Onnagh, rubbing it between my fingers to smell it better. The scent is strange. Like nuts, but not quite. I taste it. I like it. I rub some more into the skin of my hand. "It is a gift for me."

"Can you not see what is wrong here, Morragh?"

I look at my sister in confusion. There is nothing wrong here. I like this oil. I think it will be good for me. And my baby. Not that Guy-us, the giver of the gift, the maker of the child, knows about the baby yet.

"You're helping the Calgach with his plans for our people. You are to bless us all for the fight against these invaders. And yet, you are…" I feel her seeking for words that are not too cruel or too crude, actually seeking to protect me, in this moment, from her own wrath. "You are aligning yourself with one of them, one who could do much harm to us all, one who could undermine any plan we have, especially if you go telling him anything about it."

I smile and shake my head. I know her concerns hold no validity.

"It's betrayal, Morragh. Treachery. You are Taezali. Or are you a woman of Rome, now?'

"I am Morragh," I say, and turn from her, retreating to my room.

She follows. "What does that even mean, anymore? You are not the same person you were before you were... before you met that man!"

This is not true. Not exactly. "I am more," I tell her and it is her turn to walk away, shaking her head as she does so.

Later I put the nutty oil on my food. Onnagh refuses to take any. And then I rub it into my belly as I lie in bed. I dream sweet dreams that night. Dreams of Guy-us, his eyes bright and laughing, how he would be in a life with no worries. Actually, this is how he is at a time of great worries. I am laughing with him in the dream, and dancing too. We are in a hot place, a city. It seems odd to me with its huge stone buildings built all in straight lines, and its people: so many people. The scents of the place are overwhelming, but the deep smell of the oil is woven through it all, familiar and enchanting. People, people, everywhere, and all that goes along with so many living so close together. It is too much. Too busy and overwhelming. So we head away from the city, out into the green places and we are happy.

It is a true dream, but the events the vision depicts are a long way off. Because, in the dream, we are old. Guy-us and Morragh are grey and wrinkled and thin.

I wake with the thought: we have lots to do here first. Lots is not a big enough word. So much. Too much? No. But it will be hard. So hard. Too hard? Yes. No. I do not know all of it yet. None of us do.

There's something extra coming. Something strange and terrible. Unimaginable. So I don't try. To imagine. Because first? Before any of that? First there is a time of

90

gentle love and fun and laughter. Between now and High Summer, that is all that is to come, I hope, I think, and it is all I let myself believe.

I sing as I hang our washed clothes on a rope between two trees, because I know that he is near. The oil was only the beginning of this phase, and this is a time to be treasured for all the secret sweetness it brings.

I take cheese and dried berries from our store, and some fresh baked bread too. He will bring more. Food of the Sons of Mars. I know it. But I will have to lead us somewhere safe before we can meet openly in the broad light of day. He is close and I hope he will follow. I sing his name into my song of love and laughter and dancing, so he will know to follow, and off I skip through the trees, with the food wrapped in a blanket. I go deep into the forest, not in the direction of Cullykhan but more towards Taexali point, though that would not be a good place to go, for it is too well seen from both sea and land, bared of trees and high up as it is.

I find the perfect place. It is protected by a large oak who I thank for its presence, here in this small glade. The Goddess is all about, a bright and sunny aspect of Her who delights in love between people, any people, all people; she makes no distinctions such as Taezali and Rome.

I spread the blanket on the ground and lay the food on a flat stone to the side. Maddagh gave me the best bread this morning, the one dotted all through with little black seeds.

We will enjoy it.

We will enjoy everything.

I lie on my side on the blanket and wait. I feel like giggling but I do not, for there is a sacred element to today and this meeting too. We are bound to one another, Guy-us and I. We were born far apart but put in this place together at this time to… to what? Something nags… something wants to be spoken. "To change the world." Really? We are that big?

Yes.

We are that big.

We are all that big.

And we all change the world every day as we go about making choices, taking action, sitting still and most of all: by adding more love into the places around us. This is highest. This is best.

He is here. He makes no sound and does not move the blanket even the tiniest bit, but I know he lies beside me now. I long to see him but I keep my eyes closed. I want to savour him, his presence, and everything I can notice and feel without sight first.

He smells of the oil he gave me. I love that smell. I cannot help but smile even though there is still no sight, no sound and no touch. But the anticipation of these things is great, between us both. I can feel his breath now as we are so close. And then it is too much for Guy-us who kisses me on the mouth, awakening all the energies that have been waiting. My eyes fly open as I jump right onto him, legs either side as if he were a horse, though I am not on his back. Of course not.

His eyes are just like they were in the dream, full of love and laughter. And this is our time. We love like that, with me on high, we cannot wait; the yearning we have for each other is too great. And I think what an amazing thing this joining of human bodies is, how we fit together this way and how it feels. I never understood the feelings of it before. The rituals of summer and winter are sacred in more ways than I had been able to comprehend. The magic of this act is intense and powerful. Each time I meet with Guy-us, I learn more.

After, as we lie together on the forest floor, in a state of breathless relaxation, I guide Guy-us's hand to my belly which is already fatter than it used to be. At first he is only happy: a baby of Guy-us and Morragh, us two making three and it is a simple joy. It's a joy that has been experienced by people through all the time of our existence in this world. But then I see a shadow pass over his face, caused by a thought about how this might not be so simple, and not so easy; I see him travel down a straight and very direct road of thoughts that threaten to lead him away from our sunny loving day.

"No," I command. "This is us here today. And that's all that should be." And I crawl away from him and over the blanket to fetch the food, the best bread and cheese and berries.

Guy-us has brought food too, as I knew he would. Meat, this I recognise. It is cooked and a little tough, but salty and good. He also brings strange dense oily berries. Ah! They are the source of the oil. I like them so much. I could eat them forever.

He speaks as we eat. I like to listen to his voice and his language. But he has learned some of ours! I am amazed and delighted to hear him use our words. And I do understand what he is asking of me. That I might stay far away from any confrontation or battle.

I shake my head. I cannot promise him this. Other than the fate of the Calgach, I have not sensed or been shown the details of what is to pass on that day for the rest of us.

"You will be there," I say, knowing this one thing to be true, and pressing my finger into his chest to press my point forward.

"Aye, Morragh," he says, and I laugh at the way he says it, the pronunciation changed and different from how I am used to hearing both words. And then, I understand the meaning of the rest he says in his own tongue as he uses his hands to gesture too: he has to be there. I do not.

"I will help the Calgach," I say simply. "I will do what I need to do."

"The Calgach? Calgacus?" His eyes are wide and his words loud. This is a shock to Guy-us.

"He is my friend," I say, hand over my heart. "But not my… lover," I add, smiling, pushing Guy-us down to the ground and kissing him again to make this clear.

He understands. He knows.

And he does not ask me about the Calgach again.

The glade becomes our place. Too far from Stane Hame for any Taezali to wander through it. Too far from the bases of Rome for those marching men to ever see it. They don't march into the thick of the forest. Only Guy-us journeys through the trees, unseen. We meet in the bright light of the forest almost every day. Sometimes with food, sometimes without, for we are both so keen to run here, to get here.

To be here with each other.

This is the sweet time. The time in between. And we revel in it. We roll around and shout and scream in it.

When I am not with Guy-us, I want to be. I think about him all the time. Or I feel the feeling of him, his brightness, his smile; they live in me. Intimate memories spring to mind at strange times when they probably should not. His kiss. His mouth on my neck. His body, all the different parts and places of it.

My face shows the content of my mind to the one who knows me best. Onnagh knows. Not any of the sweet details. But she knows I meet him. And she is not pleased about it. She shakes her head and her mouth goes straight as she looks upon me with some crossness, but my joy is so great that I can usually get her to smile.

I use a technique that I employed in childhood when Onnagh was sad. Sometimes I sensed great sorrow in her, though she always did her best to hide it from me. My sister lost much when she saved me, and she can never get it back. More than anything she missed her mother, when we were little, when we were children.

As I did then for her sadness, now I work on her anger. I make my face look funny. I open my eyes wide – so wide – I make them huge. And I make my mouth tiny, lips all scrunched together, so small. I tilt my head and look at Onnagh, and I do not blink.

"Stop it, Morragh. We are not bairns now. Morragh, do you hear me? I said, stop…" Her voice may still sound cross, but it is a pretence. Because she has smiled. Sometimes she even laughs.

And soon, it is not just Onnagh who knows of my meetings in the forest.

***

One moment I am all alone as I walk through the trees to meet Guy-us. The next, I am not alone. I am watched. I am seen.

I smell her before I see her, the great Mother Bear. She has sensed me too, for she shows no surprise when I encounter her beside a great oak, the darkness of the woods around us hiding both her and me, making us invisible, at least to those who should not know.

At first the space between the trees is only dark, but then the brightness of her eyes reveals her presence. Two sparks in the gloam, and finally her whole furry self emerges from the vegetation, lumbering and large, like a great bear Goddess of story and legend.

I bury my face in the fur of her neck and she nuzzles my hair. There is huge love here in us for one another. We have missed each other. I am so lucky. I have always had love. And now I only have more.

I want her to follow me. And she does.

I want her to meet Guy-us. And he is there, in the glade, before us.

He is lit up with happiness when he first sees me, but then he cringes, he bends at the knees, and he becomes fierce. He reaches for his knife. It is in his hand as he commands that I get behind him. And the Mother Bear? She does not like it.

They want to fight each other. They want to hurt each other. No. No. This is not how it should go. I will not let it. Birds fly from the treetops in a rush as I shout for Guy-us and the bear to calm down, to know that it is safe, and that they should be quiet and still.

She roars, standing like a giant man, waving her arms in fury. He leaps forward, to stab, to kill, and it is him that I grab, him that I stop.

The knife falls to the ground as he tries to get me to run, to flee with him to safe places. I pick the weapon up and throw it into the trees. She knows it is an object of danger. She knows it can hurt and kill. And it is making her angry.

Defying Guy-us, I shrug free of his grip, and turn to the bear, reaching out both my hands to her, making soothing noises of old, noises she used to make to me when I was wee and lost and cold.

"Take my hand, Guy-us," I say, without looking round at him, but reaching my hand back for him to hold. I do not dare take my eyes off the Mother. She is back down on all fours now, but she could still scare and flare with rage.

He does not obey me at first. For a short moment I think he will flee and leave me here to die from what he sees as my complete foolishness. But of course he does not. He would die with me. That is the risk he takes; as his fingers curl round mine, it is the risk he believes he is taking.

He would protect me. He tried to. And now I have shown myself unwilling to be protected? He chooses to die here with me instead. There is an echo of the future in the actions of the present. But I cannot look there.

He comes forward with me, though he does not touch her, the bear. Not as I do. In fact, not at all.

She sniffs all the space around him, and does not touch him either.

They regard each other, these two, these precious two.

Then she knocks my chin up with her nose and wanders away into the forest, crashing through the undergrowth as she goes this time, wanting her presence and strength to be known. But she approves of my mate. And I know that she is aware of our baby too.

I smile at Guy-us and say: "My Mother."

"Mother," he repeats, looking disbelieving. It is clearly one of the growing number of words he understands.

"Aye, Guy-us," I say, laughing now at his disbelieving expression.

"Daughter of bear?"

"Son of Mars?"

"Aye, Morragh." And then we are laughing, smiling, bright and happy, back to our usual selves together. Though he glances into the trees many times that day, bringing a small amount of fear into the glade, I am glad that he has met her, my Mother, the bear.

A Newly Forged Sword

There is a bright bustle of life when I arrive back at the great round house of Stane Hame, late in the day. People are busily going here and there, smiling at me as I walk among them. I wonder where Onnagh is, and I also wonder if she saw me leave this morning. And I wonder, too, at this general brightness. We all know there is great peril ahead. Yet, all I hear people discussing is the fact that what has happened in the lower lands has not happened here; there has been no butchery or rape such as the Calgach spoke of. In truth, I have heard words like this spoken around our settlement often in the last weeks, though I do not always listen to idle words. Listening to what lies behind them is usually better.

I am glad nobody is linking the Long Night, and me, and my pregnancy, to the Sons of Mars. The only emotions that have been expressed about the baby are joy and wonder, and that is as it should be.

I close my eyes and relax into the feeling of the busyness around me.

Ah, yes. People want to think the Calgach is invincible. That Rome will not dare attack him or his people, which now includes us, the Taezali. They want to believe that he will save them. With their help of course. Everyone is needed now. Everyone is made important now.

The people of Stane Hame are enjoying all that needs to be done, all the preparations of our daily life that seem even more vital now, from growing food to hunting and making clothes; and the other thing, the bad thing? We think not on it. Not really. Only to prepare. Not to feel it

98

yet. I, too, am the same. I am detached from the strife that the fierce aspect of the Goddess told us of in the chamber. It will come, and it is for the time that it comes. It is not for now. Not here on this brightest of days.

Loud industry is taking place at Darragh's workshop. Several other men have joined him, and they are all being industrious and important, making the sharpest of weapons.

"Do you approve, Morragh?" Darragh asks, as I run my finger along the sharp bronze blade of a new sword.

I look him straight in his eye, as is often my way now, and say: "I do." I look away again quickly, but I feel how the eye contact makes the words seem weightier somehow, how it gives them more import.

The men cheer. My voice is considered both a good omen and it is also said to be an honour when I speak directly to someone. This is patently ridiculous. It is just a voice. Equally as special as anyone else's voice. It's just Morragh's voice at this moment, not even a hint of Her in any of her forms. But even as I think that thought, the change comes.

My eyes are drawn back to the sword. I sit beside it and put my hand round its hilt. I can see it twice, both laying on the bench, newly forged and sparkling as it is on this bright and sunny day, and lying down on the ground, dropped on the wet, muddy, bloody, grassy ground. Its owner? Dead before the sword ever fulfilled its intended purpose. My eyes stay on the long sword, the metal so shiny, as people, so many people, are slain around it.

No. No to this. I am so saddened. So filled with the horror of what is to come. I do not want to take this in yet. Not today. Not here in this happy sunny day at Stane Hame.

Though, now I have seen it, I immediately plan to prepare salves, and dressings and ointments in great quantity. This will be one of my tasks.

But salves are not what matters right now. Right now I am deep in vision, deep in knowing, and I know I have to take my inner eye off the sword, and not let any part of me linger or focus on the coming battle. Or the bloody details. The suffering, the phenomenal level of suffering, is what I find hard to pass by. To ignore such a thing feels inhuman, but I know I must do it. I pull my head up fast within the vision and flick my eyes past that bloody layer of sight and sound and look up instead, up towards the horizon. To what I'm meant to see.

I'm looking up at the Great Mother Hill. So, we are beside it on the day of battle. We are on its lower slopes. I want to reject this seeing. I squirm, my hand still on the metal of the sword. The hill is sacred. It should not be defiled by blood and war. It is the great hill of our people, and others, all people. It is the curved and womanly shape of the Goddess lying upon the land. So high, so solid, so everlasting, and so safe.

So safe. Safe for some. Not for us. Not on the day of the fight.

But this is what will be. And it has to be told and known.

I shake my head free of the future images, and stand up. How best to explain this to people? I feel so much, see so much, know so much. I don't want it to come out in a confusing muddle, but words tangle in my mind as I run round the settlement looking for Alaron, for it is he who must be told first.

The hill. I can still see the hill. That image does not fade from my mind's eye. I can see its hope and its protection. I can see those that dwell within it. Or are said to. I am seeing them, so this must mean that the stories of them are true. They are not only a myth or an invention. Like the Calgach is no myth either. But the Hill Folk, the Hill Folk... I focus on them now. They are very real, and they matter very much. And I must tell of them.

Quickly.

Soon.

And – finally – I see... "Alaron!"

The tall man turns at once, smiling, so pleased that I have shouted his name. He walks towards me and takes my hands in his.

"We must reach out to the Hill Folk," I tell him.

"The Hill Folk?" he says, looking doubtful.

"They're real Alaron. I have seen it. The battle will take place on their hill, or at the foot of their hill, the place of the Great Mother."

"No," he says, as keen as I am for this to be wrong. "Why would it happen there? The Hill Folk will stay hidden from the strangers of Rome as well as they stay hidden from us. They will invite no trouble."

"Our strength is in that hill," I say, hearing the echo of Her as I speak. "The height will lessen the number of fallen. And it is said, nay, it is true, that the Hill Folk have ways of disappearing into the land. Alaron..." I see it now, so clearly. "They have tunnels such as ours, with entrances known only to them."

Alaron's eyes are on me, but his thoughts are far away. "Aye," he says. "That would make sense. They have great circles of stone over there too. I have heard that they still use them. Maybe you should be the one to reach out to these people, Morragh. To go quietly and pay homage within their stones."

I picture this happening to see if it feels right and true, and it does. But this is not something I am to do alone. It will take two of us. And one of us may find it hard to be lowly and humble in front of the Hill Folk, but he must do it.

"Can you send a message to the Calgach?" I ask Alaron, who nods and soon it is done.

The Great Circles

"I knew it to be a good idea as soon as I heard it," says the Calgach as he dismounts from his horse five days later. The ground does not quake as the big man's feet land on the earth, but he is such a block of solid muscle that it feels as if it should. He is so different from anyone I have ever seen or met before and, on this sunny day, in this different place, this feels more noticeable to me than it has been on any of our previous meetings.

"No one should be left out at this time," he says, returning my smile. "These ones from the hills can be as involved as they wish."

Our messenger to the Calgach was quick. And so were we. And so here we all are, a group made up of Alaron and men of Stane Hame, the Calgach and some of his men, and me. We are already in the vicinity of the Great Hill, met near one of the ancient circles, so much larger than our own at home. This part of the plan, the details of which are all Alaron's, will be the easier part, and we hope to make the Calgach understand the manner in which we must approach the Hill Folk, if they are to help us.

However it is not an easy idea for the large man to accept. "It is us who will help them, surely?" he says, once Alaron explains. "With our army. You will be amazed at how large we have grown, Morragh! We will cover that hill and run Rome over." This last he says with a wide smile.

"Without the Hill Folk, we will be stuck there on the slopes, whatever happens on the day," I remind him. "Trapped even. They are an ancient living people who know the old and secret ways of the hill. They do not mix with the other tribes, in fact they may not even be a tribe as we understand it. We think they honour some aspect of the Goddess within these great circles that are all around the hill, but we do not really know. Their ways are known only to themselves. You and me, Calgach, will honour Her here in one of their circles today, and then we will walk onto the hill and ask for their help."

He nods, happy enough to let me declare what will be on this day. I am impressed again. This man is used to being the one in charge, the one to say who will go where and what will be done. Yet, he lets me take the lead. In this moment, here near the Great Hill, at least.

We leave Alaron and the other men who accompanied us on our respective journeys now, and the two of us walk up the gentle slope. The Calgach manages to maintain a suitable silence as we approach the large circle of stones.

The stones are tall and wide. Perfectly placed, as always. There are many more of them than at home. Everything is larger here. I examine the place closely, with great care in fact. This seems important. I sense an extraordinarily high level of care is being given to the circle on a regular basis. By someone. Or someones.

Unseen. Hidden. Ancient.

The grass has been kept low, but there is no sign of blackened earth from fire or the scatter of white stone fragments that our own rituals tend to leave behind. I hold up a hand for us to stop, to be quiet and still, as I try to determine what it is that takes place here, and exactly what should happen today, between us and between the stones.

Nothing. That's all I get.

Quiet.

Still.

Nothing.

No. Not nothing. Just a different thing to what we are used to seeing as something. A sitting, a stilling, a casting of one's mind into the centre of the stones. I take the Calgach's hand, hoping I can take him with me into whatever wonder this sacred rite holds.

As soon as our feet touch the centre of the circle, it feels as if we are whirling, flying, as if our souls have taken flight away from our bodies. Round and round and through the stones. Squeezing into the tiny space between the two huge recumbents. Twin stones here. As it is a twin circle. Twin stones. Twin stones. These words, and this idea, echo on and on, determined to impress themselves on me. I try to push myself forward, and I seem to be suddenly standing right within the largest stone itself, almost as if I am part of it; it is hard and grey and strong and filled with wee lights, and so am I.

My eyes snap open and we are both still standing exactly where we were before. We are breathless in the daylight again, the Calgach's eyes wide and shocked from being inside the stone. He was with me there. I know he was.

Twin Circle. Twin Circle. I hold my hand up to lock out the bright glare of the sun, as I search the horizon back and forth and back again, and then, at last I see it. It is so well hidden, on the other side of a small valley, surrounded by trees and thick undergrowth, that I missed it on first glance. But I see the shape of the recumbent stone now, blurred with greenery as it is, and it is there, to this semi-concealed circle, that we must now go. It is the more sacred space, the more ancient.

Still we are quiet. Still we don't speak. This is important, and it is instinctual. To him as it is to me.

We hold hands as we walk down and then up the short grassy valley that lies between the two circles. The stones we arrive at are overgrown with all manner of plant life.

There are healing herbs that I recognise, wee flowers too, and spiny stems that look rather forbidding. Keep out, they say. Stay away. Leave the stones in peace. There are creatures here as well. I sense them before I see them. A mouse shoots out of the green growth, looks at us and then shoots back in.

I look at the Calgach and smile. He smiles back and seems almost on the brink of speaking. But we must not. Not here. Not yet. A small movement of my head conveys this and he understands at once. It would be irreverent to utter words here, visitors, even intruders, as we are. It would scare those we hope to reach. Perhaps not scare. That notion seems wrong. But they would choose not to approach us, not to let us in, if we could not grasp the simple need for silence here in this space. We have not been welcomed in, not accepted, and I feel it is still undecided as to whether we will be.

I stay still as we wait, but let my eyes examine and assess every aspect of the stone circle that I can see through the plants. The stones are smaller than those we have just come from, across the valley, smaller than those of Stane Hame too. There is a gentle pinkness to them that I love. I see quickly that this circle is no longer complete. The recumbent and one flanker remain upright and in place. Others have fallen and been grown over. Nature has wrapped herself round these beautiful stones, round and round and round them, as if to weave a covering. They are all but invisible, and I know not to try what we did with our minds in the other circle. That is not what this place is for. This is something else altogether.

There's the smallest rustle. But not that of a mouse.

The voice that comes is soft, a little raspy, but gentle and, I feel, kind. "You have found us, Morragh of the Stone People," says a small and ancient man who looks like a natural extension of the circle itself, wrapped in greenery as he is and having just appeared out of the vegetation.

I do the only thing to be done, and I pull on the Calgach's hand to make sure he does it too.

We kneel.

The Hill Folk

We stay there, kneeling, for a long time. The wind blows around us as we both keep our eyes down, looking only at the ground. I feel the stare of the old one as he assesses us, and it is like nothing I have ever felt before. The only sensation I can liken it to is when I am alone in our stones at home; sometimes it is as if a breeze from the past blows through the place, and I catch the energy of a time come before. Before now. Long before.

Finally something shifts. And the man speaks.

"Look at me," he says, and I fully behold the oldest being I have ever seen. He is small and bent with grey hair hanging loose down beyond his waist. He is naked apart from the plant life that clings to him as it does the stones. "The man of war must remain here," he says, holding out an arthritic looking hand to me.

"Wait here," I tell the Calgach.

He murmurs back, as if in a dream: "I will wait here."

I am within the overgrown circle with the old one now, holding his hand tightly like a wee bairn might do for guidance and help. The plants pull and tug at me and my clothing as I move. For a moment I feel panic as the greenery seems to be deliberately tearing and poking my clothes and skin with thorns and sharp stems.

"Don't fight," says the old man. "Let the place take you in."

I breathe slowly and move slowly and the plants give way, their touch changing to be more like a caress or a greeting as the old one speaks again.

"You have been in deep places before, Morragh of the Stone People. Prepare to go deeper."

It is like the tunnel to the chamber. But also not like it. He is right. This is deeper. Wilder. More fiercely natural. There are no carved or placed stone steps here, just a way that feet have made within the world, a path of sorts. There is stone at both sides but also earth, softer and quieter than stone, beneath my feet. It feels warm in places, colder in others, and I am lulled by this warm and cool and warm and cool effect for a long while before we stop.

Like in the chamber at home, we are in darkness but not quite; there is light, though it is just barely discernible. This is not the light and air of the sea though. This is mountain terrain. Mountain subterrain. Mountain earth and light.

And now we have arrived at a larger space. It is not just me and the old one who are here now. I cannot see them yet, but I know that there are others. Many? A few. And they are inspecting me, deciding something, walking round and round me. My eyes and other senses catch hints of them now and then, and I feel a prickling sensation on my arms and the back of my neck. I shiver.

A light appears. I see it and focus on it for a moment, because I know it has been lit specially for me, to allow me to see them. The Hill Folk. All of them. I smell the animal fat from the lamp and lift my eyes to see many more people, all of them elderly in the extreme, all of them wizened and bent with age like the first one, the one that guided me here. They are all unclad like him too, some of them wearing bits of greenery about their persons, some not. Their eyes are bright, though narrowed against the light. I was right. The lamp is only for me, to make me feel safe and welcome. They neither need nor want it.

"It is Morragh," says the first old one. "She has come to us."

I hear my name being said among them quietly, but I do not know the language they speak. It is not like ours, nor is it like the words spoken by Guy-us. Again I know I am hearing something deeply old, a language of the hills from long before the Taezali were ever here.

"You keep alive the old ways," says a woman, stepping forward and peering at me. "Why?"

"Because it must be so," I say.

The woman speaks again. "You think you bring new ways to the ancient chamber in the earth, but you do not. It was ours before it was yours, and men entered too in the old times."

I nod. I had sensed this. I do not ask how they know about the new change. It does not seem right to do so. They will tell me what I need to know.

"You are right to call the chamber a womb," she says. "It is for birthing the new. This is why we left. It was no longer for us. Maybe it is for you. What do your people call us?"

"The Hill Folk."

A murmur of mirth passes through the group.

"We are the Old Ones, the people of the earth," she says. "We came with the fire."

She reaches forward and places her hand over my heart. I see the earth, moving and pulsing, a great force of melted stone flowing along as a red fiery river and then slowing, setting into hard cold stone. Then ice. Ice moves all around the fiery land, sculpting the sides until it is recognisable as the Great Mother Hill that we know in this time. I admired the shape of the hill often as I rode with Alaron to meet the Calgach this morning. It appeared through trees and over brows of hillocks again and again, a great master of the landscape.

"Mistress maybe," says the woman, seemingly having divined my thought. "Its secrets will die with us."

And I realise: there are no children. Every one of these people, this community, has come to meet me. There are no others hidden away. The Old Ones are all actually old, older than old, and though their lives are long, they will not live forever.

"So what do you ask of us, Morragh of the Stone People?" the old woman asks now.

"I ask for your help in a battle."

"We will play no part in the fights of the young."

"Will you aid our people in escape after it is done? It is to take place on the slopes of the Great Mother Hill. I have seen it."

The Old Ones huddle closer in, all around me, interested, curious and something else: knowing. And then I am being touched. Gently, gently, like being brushed by many breezes or plants at once. They are exploring me, keen to know more of me. It is strange. They like my hair and my feet and my clothing. The woven fabric is strange to them, and they study it with their hands and noses. And all at once, the movement, the touching, stops.

I am still.

Everything is still.

The woman who was talking before now places her hand on my belly and looks at me in consternation, as if sensing some strangeness. She shakes her head free of it, whatever it was, and tells me: "We have no new ones now. Our ways will be closed off when we are gone. Even the womb. You are only a temporary guardian, Morragh."

"Show her." The words seem to be said by many around us in whispering echoes, and I follow the old woman out of the wider space and through into a different earthy narrow one. We walk some way, unspeaking, and then, stones are shifted, pulled back or pushed from the side by persons unseen. It is confusing. But the shifting stones have created a gap in the inner wall of the

111

mountain, almost like my window at home but even more unusual than that. We are suddenly looking out from the hillside of the Great Mother Hill. We are looking down, down the slopes, so beautiful, brown with heather and grey with stones that are flat in places, making me think of the chamber.

"Look beyond," she breathes, and I do. I look across miles of land. I see more hills and the flatter places beyond, and then a camp comes into view and it is huge. There are lines and lines of tents, like we would have for a gathering. But also not like. These are all the same, each one identical to the next. And the lines are perfectly straight lines. Just like the sturdy wooden fences that guard the camp, all around the perimeter. Fierce and sharp stakes of wood, determined and forbidding.

And the men. The men of Rome. The Sons of Mars. They are everywhere. There's not hundreds of them. No. There's more. So many more. I do not have words for the number of men I see. All men. No women. They are the army that will fight us. The Calgach will lead us against these men.

Men more than words.

Men more than space.

Men more than have ever been here in these lands before.

As fast as the strange window to the hill opened, it is closed again, stones pushed back in place, and we are moving, returning back down the way we came. I feel I cannot cope. I am overwhelmed. My head is full of numbers I do not know, quantities of people I have never envisioned before, and it is too much.

The woman places her hands on my shoulders and we stand still and breathe, just breathe, until I feel calm again, and then she leads me back to the open area. The other Old

Ones have backed off, quietly, quietly, but they are still there and they are discussing.

I am alone for a while. A long while. Deep within the earth while the bright day passes by on the surface. I feel at peace. And old. And young. And quiet. I like the dark I have been left in. I could come to know these ways, to live in these ways.

"Our ways are not your ways, Morragh," says the woman, coming closer again. "But we will offer you and your people escape." And I understand that this is a decision that has been made by them all. This is it. This is what they will give us. The woman speaks on. "Those that can run to the top of the hill, the Mither Tap, will be guided to safety. It will be our last involvement in the human matters of this world and perhaps our greatest. Many lives will be preserved in this way. And perhaps we will also live on in your stories and legends of the dark day that is to come."

"If I can make it so, you will," I promise. "And thank you."

"We thank you too, Morragh of the Stone People, for coming to us this day. And now, our youngest will lead you back."

The man I met in the overgrown circle appears again, showing what I think is a smile in the dimness. As we walk, I tell him about the High Summer ritual that we have planned. I tell him that he and all his people would be welcome to attend. He does not answer. I am sure it is not something they would normally do, or wish to be a part of. But it is right to ask them, to involve and include and respect them, these Old Ones of the earth. I find my voice babbling like water in a stony stream as we retrace our steps through the soft floored tunnels, telling him the details of our practice in the Circle at Stane Hame. He is like a rock to my wee river, solid and quiet, but I think he likes hearing of our ways, though he is unused to hearing chatter such as mine. This thought is strange to me, Morragh, who did not used to speak, and we both laugh as I think it.

Soon I am stepping back out into the overgrown circle, wading through the plant growth and then squinting through bright sunlight at the waiting, still kneeling, Calgach.

Dragon Pin

"The Rite of High Summer is more important than ever now," says the Calgach, as our wee group traverses the side of a small loch.

The place is beautiful. Surrounded by silver birch trees, all newly in green leaf, the sunlight sparkles on the surface of the water as a heron flies over. But the Calgach sees none of this. High Summer is all that is in his mind, all that he can see, hear or speak about. He has been totally fixated on the subject since we rode away from the great circles and the Great Mother Hill some hours ago.

I am seated right behind him, on his huge brown horse, so that we can talk easily, but it is as if he doesn't want to know about anything that I learned while I was below ground with the Hill Folk. Rather than discuss the enormous number of men that is the army of Rome, as Alaron was keen to do when he rode up alongside, or even where those men are camped and what they might be doing or planning, the Calgach just talks on and on about High Summer and all the details of the gathering and ritual.

I understand. I think I do anyway, as we ride along, the movement of the horse keeping time with my thoughts, or so it feels. Pacing them. Letting them come naturally. High Summer is an easier subject. A happier subject. I know this man that I hold on to now is keen to fight for his people, and willing to die for his people on that day, but he is holding it off for now. War is not today. War lies beyond High Summer, so beyond High Summer he will not look. Not yet. For now, everything must stay sunny and bright. Like this day. Warm and safe and companionable.

We pass out of the bright evening sunshine and through a thick patch of forest, the world darkening around us, the air rich with the smell of damp earth and old wood and moss and lichen. The Calgach's thoughts venture to deeper, darker places too, as he continues to talk on and on.

"All who wish it may be blessed in the chamber," I confirm, once there is space in his speech for me to do so, his need to impress upon me the importance of the mass blessings so intense that I did not like to interrupt.

"And what will the blessings be like for them?" he asks. "I know it will not be as it was for me."

"How it will be is not for me to decide," I tell him. "It will be different for each one. These things always are. But, usually, a blessing is a happy, relaxed experience."

"And the gathering at the stones?" he says. "I know it is ancient and sacred. Is it truly powerful though, Morragh? Will everyone feel it?" I sense he is looking for anything hopeful he can pass on to his warriors.

I nod as we ride. "It is a quieter event than the winter one. We watch the sun set and rise, and then we feast."

"So it is not a ritual of mating, of men and women?'

"Some do celebrate this way; they go off into the woods."

"And you and me, Morragh? We will do this?"

"We will not, Calgach," I state with some firmness, but my mouth forms a small smile despite my tone. For the first time I can imagine what it would be like to take part in this aspect of the rite. I mean, if Guy-us were nearby on that night… but no. Of course not. My smile fades. The danger would be too great.

"No need to frown, Morragh," says the Calgach, looking round at me. "I was speaking in jest."

"I know," I tell him. "Thoughts of the danger we are in, that we are all in, surround me."

"Focus on High Summer instead," he advises, and does just this himself, ceaselessly, all the way home, filling my head with talk of the story-tellers and entertainers and musicians that he intends to invite.

As soon as we arrive at Stane Hame, I dismount from the beautiful horse, and run to the wee hoose for the peace and quiet and stillness of it. My head is buzzing with the incessant chatter of the Calgach, and I wonder if the Hill Folk felt this way when I left, especially their 'youngest'. I did rather talk on and on to him on the way back to the circle. I now need to think and feel and sense all I can about what I was told by those people of the earth, and all that I saw, and to contemplate the very nature of the Hill Folk themselves.

More of us will live because of what these old and ancient living people are willing to do. And that is good. But I have seen the army. I have seen the size of that army. And it could grow bigger yet. In fact, it definitely will. So I know, without any doubt, that many of our people will not live. The battle that is to come will shrink the number of the Taezali greatly. And the other tribes too, of course, but I cannot focus that wide and that far today, not on this, the subject of death. In that I am like the Calgach. I will only look so far.

By the time I rejoin the Taezali for the evening meal, the Calgach has already told them that the Old Ones are to help us on the day, at the end of all that is to happen on that day, by offering safe passage through the hill. And it is only then, as I bite into some bread, that I understand more of what this day was like for him.

I hear him telling Onnagh about what he observed of the Great Mother Hill, how the light changed with the sun and how clouds travelled quickly above in the sky, casting shadows across the brown slopes of the hill as they went.

He had to stay by the overgrown circle, a deeply unusual and special place, all by himself for a long time, not knowing when, or even if, I was returning. He remained kneeling, not wanting to show any disrespect. Strong and tall he may be, but staying for so long in the same position must have been tiring. He had to be patient, and quiet, not states of being that are innate to him, and the main view in the line of his sight was the place that will be the scene of his death. Sometime after summer he will die on that hill, along with so many of his friends and companions.

So he doesn't dwell on it. He knows what has to be done; I have no doubt he will strategise and plan well for the coming events. But, for now, he lets his mind wander through, and stay fixed on, the delights of High Summer, and why should he not? He is right. We must make it a day and night of joy to remember for as long as we live. Or for as short a time as we live, as it will be for some. For many.

Indeed, I also cannot bear to contemplate the full force of that dark day that is to come, the battle and all it entails. I look at Onnagh and Alaron, and Jarredd who is come to visit, and it is too terrible to think, not so much that they will die for that will come to us all one day after all, but that they will suffer.

And they will.

We all will.

Alive or dead, injured or unscathed, each one of us will be changed so fiercely by these times we are living through, that we will be barely recognisable by the end of them.

And this is the last time we will be together like this. These months now, are to be celebrated. These people here now are to be loved and cherished, for soon so many will be gone. Or changed. Or saddened.

"Cheer up, Morragh," says Onnagh, standing and leaning across the table to me. "Another gift was left for you." Bright red sparks of annoyance emanate from my sister as she passes the small object over to me. I have never seen anything quite like it, but it delights me as much as it angers her. I turn the thing in my hands as Onnagh explains to the Calgach that people sometimes leave gifts for me, and that this habit has increased recently.

It is a dragon, a bit like the one on my wrist. But this one is on a pin. Immediately I think I will be too scared to wear it, for fear of the pin coming loose and the dragon falling away into the grass and being lost forever. But this is the time we have for joy and thanksgiving. If it falls, another will find it sometime and delight in it too, and so the world goes on.

Jarredd asks to see the pin and examines it with great interest. He turns it over to look at the clasp and then stares intently at the front, the dragon design.

Onnagh glares at me as he does this.

"It's strange," says Jarredd, rubbing his fingers over the ornate metal shapes and lines of the piece. "It's our dragon, but worked in a different style to any I have seen. It's unusual and beautiful, Morragh. You have a keen admirer, I think? One who has seen your arm band and knew you would like this?"

I smile my answer to Jarredd.

"May I see?" asks the Calgach, then taking his turn inspecting my gift.

"This has come from down south," he declares. "I have seen such things before. It is in the style of Rome but using our dragon, our artwork. Their mark is wider than the enslavement and rape that no one can fail to notice. The

119

metalwork of the land is changing too. Our way of life, our customs, these are all in danger of being wiped out, as are we ourselves."

He hands my gift back.

I pin it to my wrap, close to my heart. It helps to hold the garment in place. Onnagh, Jarredd and the Calgach watch me.

And then, I join my people in planning the greatest High Summer Ritual that any of us will ever remember.

Sea of Tents

I stand on the grass surrounded by the tents of the men of Rome. It is as if I am deep in vision. But I am not. This is all very real and happening right now here at Stane Hame. These are tents made to house an army of warriors. They at once intrigue and repel me. Intrigue, for this is what Guy-us must sleep in at night, sometimes at least, when he is not abroad in the wild by himself. Repel, because, these are objects of war, of dominion and travel with the aim of conquest. A conquest of blood and pain. Rape and butchery are the hallmarks of those who made and sleep in these tents, as the Calgach has reminded all of us so many times.

But the men of Rome are just that: men. Men who need sleep like any other men, and in sleeping they are as vulnerable as children. These sloping roofs will not protect them should they be attacked.

The tents are made of thin animal skin, and they move gently in the air, making it seem that I am cast adrift in a strange sea of things to come. The event that we rarely speak or think of, the battle we are all to face, is somehow echoing all around me now.

"Are they not magnificent?" asks the Calgach, striding towards me through the camp, his hair loose and flowing back in the breeze today. He looks like the God of this sea, this great ocean, strong and invulnerable and beautiful.

"Do you want to know how we got them?" he asks.

In fact, I had not stopped to wonder how these tents came to be the visitors' accommodations for High Summer. I was just interested to see them. I understood they had solved a big problem. We need to spend time preparing weapons, not building temporary shelters for guests. And then, here, these tents appeared just when they were needed.

"The Caledones have raided the camps of Rome more than a few times," the Calgach tells me now, with that wide smile of his. "And we never come away empty handed. Look." He reaches into the pockets of his trews and withdraws many coins. They are strange like the tents, as I look at them and hold them. The small metal discs are shiny with the heads of men who have been made important on them. These are the men who play games of war and conquest. But these are not the men who will fight or die in those games. There we differ from Rome. Our leaders will be among us in the fullness of the fray. The heads on these coins? They will stay in their grand and shiny stone houses, eating the oily little fruits that I have come to love. These metal men are not in any danger. Not on the battlefield anyway. There is other danger for them from their own people. I sense strange games are played all around them. They know it. They accept it. There is even thrill in it for them.

The Calgach shakes his handful of coins, making a merry jingling sound, bringing my mind home from the large stone buildings and grand leaders of Rome. "What do you think we can make with these?" he asks, and his face is all twinkly and happy, and I am glad for him. He is like a naughty wee child playing an innocent game, not like the ones played by the coin men.

"I think that you will show me," I say.

"I will, Morragh, but not yet. You will have to wait and see."

It is three days later until I see what he means. But before then, I see the sleeping quarters of Rome transform into the dwellings of the tribes. There is nothing of the

Sons of Mars left about them anymore. And none of it feels much like the Taezali either. I walk through a wild meadow of bright flowers when I wander through the camp now, rather than an ocean. There are flowers tied to the tents and paintings put right on to them, right there on the animal hide: swirls and circles and suns, and – oh yes! – there's even a tent that has become a huge rainbow.

The peoples, the tribes, are here in all their colourful loud glory. And their ways are different than ours. I can feel how they see us, as old and staid, too quiet and not understanding the new ways of the world. This is not true of course. We, the Stone People, understand but choose to keep the old ways also. And all these people are here to see it. To join us within the stones this year. But we probably do seem a lot quieter than our visitors. For we are in our home, not on our travels and full of the excitement and interest, and noise, that that brings.

A wee bairn runs past, wearing only painted blue swirls, laughing and giggling straight into the arms of his mother. I watch them, mother and child, and feel strangely disconnected from the scene as I place my hand over my own belly, my own child. This closeness that I observe, this is not how it will be for my baby and me as parent and child. I feel a pulling away, a change, and know that our future will be different, very different, from the scene in front of me.

"You've to come, Morragh." Onnagh is cross, and I can tell that she has looked for me everywhere, and here I am, standing staring at mothers and babes among the visitors. "The Calgach told you to meet him. At midday. By the pool."

Oh yes. He was excited about it, a mischievous glint in his eye as he asked me to meet him there. High Summer is so close now. We should all be resting, but this year all there is, is busyness. The day before the event will be filled with blessings in the chamber. And there is still much planning I have to do for the ritual itself. And now this, another happening, another distraction.

Onnagh and I are not the only ones headed towards the pool. The whole community and all the many guests are all making their way down to the path that runs past our small home. They will not all fit around the water. I feel panicked about this fact. I do not understand why we are all going this way, and it is perturbing. I like to know what's happening, preferably before it happens, but at the very least while it is happening. This lack of knowledge makes me want to run and hide.

But we all walk the paths we have chosen: this path through the woods, and this path to war, and I cannot run and hide from either of them now.

There is already a crowd by the pool. I cannot see the water for them. The trees are so green with new growth, so brightly green, and waving gently in the breeze above the people, but I cannot see the Calgach. What is this gathering, but a mess of confusion and noise and nonsense?

"It's Morragh. It's Morragh." The murmur passes around the crowd, and I am glad for their joy at my arrival, though they do stare. I am finding that particularly hard on this day. The Goddess is not shadowing me, not lending her power. This is just a very human happening, involving a great many humans, and I wish it were finished and done with.

The people part for me, separating like a river round a stone, and it is to the large flat stone in the pool that my eyes are drawn. There, right on top of it, stands the Calgach, wide legged, smiling just as widely, and welcoming me, holding out a hand in my direction.

I go to wade into the water but before my feet can touch the wet, I am lifted and spirited across by a man of the Caledones. He places me on the flat-topped stone where I grab the Calgach's hand for balance, and everyone cheers as he puts his arm round my shoulders.

"Here we stand," he says, so loud and so clear, so that all may hear him. And there are people to hear everywhere. The trees are heavy with their clinging bodies, so keen are they to see this spectacle. "Morragh and the Calgach!" he continues, his voice made even greater by the flatness of the silvery pool. "The two leaders of this great pack. People of stone and metal, together, united against the tyranny of Rome."

I am truly not in an amicable mood today, and am not pleased to be described in this way. I am not the leader of Stane Hame. Alaron is, along with Alara. But he is in the crowd, not on the rock. And Alara is not here at all. The Calgach draws breath again, and I fervently hope he is not going to launch into one of his especially long speeches, for I am tired and longing for some time alone.

"This woman, who knows the ways of Spirit, who is blessed by both the Mother and Father," he says, raising my arm, "will tomorrow pass those blessings to all that want them in the sacred chamber of the Taezali!"

This news is met with more cheers, though I think everyone knew this fact already. And it's all the more reason for me to rest now, for I will be up all night preparing, and busy all day tomorrow meeting and blessing every person here.

But the Calgach is nowhere near finished yet. "Morragh leads your spirits," he tells the crowd. "As I lead your bodies, and together we know your hearts!"

Onnagh is now being carried across the pool by the large Caledone man. Given how much she loves to swim, this seems utterly ridiculous. Gone is her crossness from earlier though; she has nothing but smiles for both me and the Calgach now. No, not nothing but. She has something else too. Two somethings. Onnagh removes the shiny objects from the folds of her clothing, and holds them high in the air. The cheering is louder now, but the sun will not let me see what the things are. It illuminates them both so brightly that they dazzle my eyes, and that dazzling effect then sparks and flashes all over the surface of the water between us and the masses of people.

My sister turns to those masses now and addresses them. "Wherever the Calgach has met with Rome, he has come away the victor with many spoils. Our people have melted down the coins of the invaders, and our own great artist Jarredd has created beautiful jewellery from them. Now to our two leaders, I present a massive mark of their standing in the eyes of the people, and in the heart of the Goddess!"

She hands one of the objects to the Calgach, but he does not keep it. He takes my hand and pushes the thing up my arm, right onto the fleshy part at the top where it fits perfectly. It is, indeed, massive. It is heavy. Roman metal made into the art of our people. Swirled and marked with the pattern of wee eyes, I think. The thing is beautiful and I smile, possibly for the first time this day. I like the blending of Rome and Taezali, though not in the same way that the Calgach and Onnagh do.

I search the crowd for Jarredd to thank him, but it seems he is not here. Onnagh hands me the second arm band, the bigger, much bigger, one. It is, at once, obvious who this is for. I push it up the hairy arm of the Calgach, where it sits resplendent round his big muscled upper arm.

He raises both our arms high into the air again, and I find myself swept along with the energy of the people now, cheering and laughing along with everybody else as I leave the pool on the shoulders of the Calgach.

The Teller of Tales

The Ritual of High Summer has to be perfectly timed. Unlike winter where we have the fire all night, and the moon if it cares to make an appearance, summer has only the setting of the sun, and then the short time before it rises again. If it's cloudy, it's harder to see these exact moments, but I can always sense them.

I use my old stick to dig a hole in the centre of the Circle. Into it goes the ancestor stone. It will stay here until it is needed. Holding its knowledge. Growing in power as the sun sets and rises over the earth. The large segment of white quartz rock, to be used in the ritual, already sits atop the great recumbent, the muckle stane. Alaron found the shiny rock some months ago, and it is ready and waiting now, absorbing the light, preparing for its part in the proceedings.

There are clouds now visible between the stones as I walk them. Little puffy white clouds that appear and disappear as I stand in different places in the Circle. Here one tops a stone. Then it floats above. Safe up there in the skies. Glowing with the sunlight behind, all bright round the edges. The pointed stones are dark against this light. Hard against the softness of the clouds. I force my mind back to the night of import, the ritual, the quartz, the timing, the people. I would rather stand here and simply contemplate nature and its beauty, but this is not the time for that.

I already know it will not be cloudy on the night of High Summer this year. I do not need to plan for such an occasion. I can see it so clearly. It is vivid in my mind. This year all will be clear and the sky will be reddened.

Reddened with what is to come.

Reddened by the heightened emotions of the people. Our people. Rome's people, all people.

Reddened by blood.

I have seen that blood in the sky today. It was yet another seeing of the approaching battle. There have been so many seeings. In the chamber. For so many souls.

Hundreds of feet walked the ancient ways today. The passage that was only walked by women, a very few select women, has been tramped and marched and ran and skipped down even, in some youthful instances, today. The path will wear out. The steps will change shape, if this habit is to continue over the years. But that feels wrong. Like it shouldn't happen. Or like it won't happen. The changes that are coming will stop it. So it is good that people ran up and down those steps today, revelling in the special nature of the place, for the blessings were a special and unique event that will not be repeated.

But my mind cannot revel anywhere. I have seen too much blood.

I have seen death.

And life.

And strangeness that I do not even want to contemplate.

I am exhausted. In all the ways a person can be exhausted. By grief. By lack of sleep. Lack of food. I could not eat today.

Onnagh tried to get me to take some bread. Between blessings. Between seeings. But I could not. And hers was the worst. The blessing. Jarredd's too. But I cannot think on it. Not tonight. I have work to do. I must focus on the rite.

All I should think of is High Summer. But my heart is full of my sister and my friend. I did not understand it anyway. What happened with Onnagh in the chamber. What happened with Jarredd. They came together. As if they were a couple. Though I knew that they were not. But I loved the feeling of it. Onnagh and Jarredd together. We all felt that joy. We were happy and smiley, and everything felt fun.

Until it didn't.

For me.

I placed my hands on their heads, and the blessing passed to them and all was well, but then it was as if they might die. The danger felt so real, so close and terrible, that I wanted to sob, but I kept my face blank. I hope. I hope they did not see a shadow of the grief I felt. And then the seeing, or feeling as is more accurate, changed, and it was as if they would most definitely live and go on to be happy together. This was a huge relief, though completely confusing.

There was a vision of fire, so hot and dangerous, all round us, flaring up brightly in many colours, consuming, burning, destroying. A shield was held up to me, so that I could not look directly into the flames. I could not see what lay on the other side of the shield. There was anger, an intense fury, that I knew, that I understood. Then a huge body of water, like a deep river, flowed through my mind to stop me getting near. Or to save me from the fire, so it felt.

And that was it. My dear Onnagh and Jarredd. Fire and water, and what? I was left no wiser as to their fate. And neither were they, for I did not tell of these things that I saw and felt. They were happy with their blessing and wandered away down to the bay at Cullykhan for a swim.

Back in the present, I press my hands into the great recumbent stone, leaning my weight on it, drawing what strength I can from it. It has a curved indent that perfectly supports my belly, as if it were made for this purpose. I love it, that indent, this stone. But I am distracted.

High Summer. I must regain my focus. It is tomorrow. Tomorrow night. It's so close now. So soon. And I am woefully unready for it. It will be so different this time with all these people. So—

"I'm told you are the one who I must speak to about telling stories here in the Circle?"

The voice is loud. Intrusive and brash. The speaker, a man, sounds somewhat annoyed with me as he speaks. I turn from the great stone to look upon this intruder, one who dares to talk in such a way here in this sacred space. And I behold more strangeness. I have never seen anyone who looks quite the way this man looks. I can't place him, though there is something familiar about his haughty face. He was not one of the blessed today. I do not feel that he is one of the tribes. In fact, I think I sense a hint of Rome about him.

"Well?" he demands, studying my face in an impatient and cross manner. "Are you the great Morragh?"

"I am Morragh."

"I am Crispus, the teller of tales of love." I have the feeling that he would have liked to add the word 'great' to his name too, but held himself back from doing so.

"Crispus?" It is a strange name, one that reminds me of another. "Crisp-us…" I repeat it, sounding it out.

"Oh," he says, dismissively. "I go here and there, among all the peoples. It helps to have a name that they can all relate to."

"You've been among the Sons of Mars," I realise, rather liking the idea of that, wondering if he might have met Guy-us, but holding myself back from asking. It is a conversation of holding back.

He shrugs rather than answering.

130

"And you named yourself?" I ask.

"An empowering thing to do," he tells me, then advising: "You should try it sometime."

"I have a name."

He ignores my statement, and makes more of his own. "I am to honour the people of Stane Hame with my tales of love. Tomorrow at High Summer. During the ritual that I am given to understand will take place here." He gestures round the stones.

I almost laugh. He is not asking. He is stating. And it cannot be.

"There will be no telling of tales during the ritual, Storyteller." I can make blatant statements too. And mine are true.

"After, then?" he says, with a sigh, but at least he is asking now.

"After," I agree at once, surprising myself in that.

He smiles now, a giant smile that seems to transform the air around him, to almost make him glow. Gone is his belligerence. No thought of sighs now. It is as if I am looking on an entirely different person to the travelling man who stood here only moments ago. This one appears to be shadowed. Like She shadows me sometimes. But it is not Her that is with this man. Nor is it the God. I don't know exactly what I am looking upon. Some aspect of Spirit to do with stories and tales and performances? It is strange. And new. And, again, distracting. Maybe we need this here in this time. Maybe this man is blessed after all.

"I will look forward to your stories," I tell him.

His smile fades as he inspects me more closely than he did before.

He raises his eyebrows and says: "You have been among the Sons of Mars too." And with that, he turns and marches out of the sacred space of the Circle, leaving me a

131

little breathless and stunned. Leaving me to my planning, on this, the eve of High Summer.

High Summer

The multitudes are gathered all around the Circle now, as they were at the pool only days ago. But it's not such a squash. There is far more space up here on the hill. Wee camps have been made in the forest; the spaces between trees are being used by groups of family and groups of friends.

As I stand silent in the centre of the Circle, I can feel the wider consequences of this time of invasion and war. All these people here are affected. Many others are too. Even those who are seemingly so indirectly involved that one would think they would not be touched in any way, are, in fact, affected. Even those not involved at all. The change in the land and the people runs through everything, everyone, every tree, every branch, every twig, shoot and bud. The arrival of the Sons of Mars has been as a stone thrown in a pool, the ripples spreading outwards in never ending circles.

Those who would otherwise never have met, have met. It started with Guy-us and I. Two people. And then it became more. Whole tribes who would have stayed forever separate and distant from one another, are learning and often appreciating each other's customs and ways and words and food.

And these things are good. These meetings are good. Despite how the world is changing around us. We will be different after. We will be less in number. But more in spirit.

But tonight, the moment we are all waiting for grows close. The sun is low. The night is ready. The stones are charged, dark against the red and pink sky, buzzing in anticipation, as is everyone here. And this year: I shall not perform the sacrifice in silence.

I shall speak.

This difference was not envisioned during my planning, though had I thought about the situation properly, and the change that has been wrought in me, it should have been obvious. Had I taken the time, and had the peace and solitude of previous years, I might have realised and practised for it. There is the irony. If I had not started speaking, my preparations would have been more thorough. But it is here, now, upon me, and I have to cope with it. I ready myself to address the crowd. It will be hard. But not as hard as it was before. Each time is a little better. I am still changing, adapting and growing. All will be well.

But first I walk. I walk the great Circle, outside the ring first, pausing at each stone for a moment of reverence. I press my hands to the smooth rock, finding comforting warmth there after the day of sunshine. Atunement. Living flesh, pulsing with the beat of life, touching stone that is also living and beating in another way. There is life within. And there is wisdom. And there is a throb of energy, gathered over time. And love. Yes, love.

The people are silent. Watching as I progress to the inside of the Circle and repeat my journey. I truly love the stones, each one different, some carved to look like part of a man, some straight and tall and true in their simplicity, honest in their mere existence in this place.

In this time.

Now.

I feel their love for me. And that is new. My sensing of it. Not the love. It's been there all along. I just didn't know. Or didn't acknowledge. And I hold on to that feeling as I move closer to the moment that I must talk. I take the strength of the tall megaliths into my being, merging with them, almost as I did in the great circle of the Hill Folk. That encounter has changed me too. That connection. Those peaceful people and their ways are influencing tonight's ceremony.

Deep breath.

I climb up onto the massive stone, less graceful than usual due to my growing belly. The recumbent is perfect and unchanging. I am aware of its shape and curves and indentations. Aware of mine too, feeling every bit of me and the stone combined as one here before the tribes.

The beautiful white quartz block placed carefully between my feet, I pick up the sickled knife, polished and sharpened this morning, and slice through the late light of the day. As I do so, I take the earlier thoughts of circular ripples on the surface of a pool, and the changes come from peoples met, and I give those thoughts form. Merging them as well. Blending everything: light, thoughts, stone, flesh, mind, words, sky, sun… they are all the total of this moment. As are all of us.

I give the thoughts sound.

I give them words.

I slice the light again and again, sending it round the Circle and out into the wider world.

All around heads are nodding, minds agreeing, eyes lit with the light; yes, this is good; we will always have more allies now, more friends to turn to, not just in times of war. Though, it is to be hoped that this is the only time of war any of us will ever know.

For some it is.

For some, there will be more.

But not for the Calgach. He knows it and stands as tall and true as the stones, and just as quiet in his knowledge. And his love for his people.

And I love him for it. For all of it. The knowledge, the bravery, the love.

I truly love him.

Not as I love Guy-us.

But also not as I love Onnagh and Alaron and Jarredd.

I reach out my hand to the great man that is the Calgach, and invite him to join me on the great stone.

There is a muted gasp from the Taezali, who know this has never been the way of it before. It is always just me, as with Yannagh before, just one stands here, and that one is only ever a woman.

The Calgach fair leaps up onto the stone, delighted to be asked. He takes my lead and we lift the shiny quartz together, right up as high as my arms will allow. And we stand, still like the stones.

The light shifts slightly and sparkles off our massive armbands. It catches my dragon band too, seeming to give life to the eyes of the piece.

Still we wait. I will know when the moment is right, the perfect time for the light of this stone and the light of the sun to be split around the Circle and around our world.

Now.

Throw it down, I think to him, and he must hear me because we fling the quartz with all our might onto the large stone between us, where it shatters with an explosion of red sparks. The shards of the stone are white, but they appear pink and blue and even green in places, and I've never seen that before. But then, the stone has never been broken by two before, at least not in living memory.

"Take your shards, your sparks," I tell everybody, realising this is the first time I have said it, which means it does not really need to be said. I am joining everyone else in the habit of speaking when it is not necessary. It does not bother me, which is also unusual; I merely feel a little amused by myself, my very human self. I find myself automatically, naturally, saying more as people take their fragments of the quartz: "Hold the Light until the sun rises again, and then be met back here."

They look up at me, at us, and I am glad, in the end, that I spoke the unnecessary words. They seem to be appreciated, and of course, there are many who have never attended this rite before, so maybe all of it was for the good.

The Calgach chooses a large pointed shard from those that landed at our feet. I crouch and take a small rounded one, one from the very centre of the stone. There is both smoothness and warmth to the shiny rock as I rub it between my fingers.

The crowd has gone, melted away into the forest and beyond. The Circle is almost empty of people now. I have always been entirely alone for this next part before. I always sat in the centre of the Circle, communing with the Goddess, holding the ancestor stone. I jump down from the recumbent stone and walk to the centre, then use my stick to retrieve the carved stone from the ground there. I brush the dusty earth from its spirals and hold it out towards my one remaining companion. He joined me on the massive stone tonight, and he joins me here too. He places his hand on top of the round black ball, an action that is so right, so perfectly right, that I know how our communion will take place this night. It will not be with a pouring of rich wine into the centre of the Circle as I usually do. Though that can happen too. This will be how it took place on the longest night, but with a different pairing.

It is right.

So it will be.

And it shall be so between the fading and rising lights of High Summer, creating as sacred a moment as ever has been in this place. Surrounded by my tall guardian stones, I lead the Calgach to the flat stone, the sacrificial slab, and there I lie with him. He is so gentle with me, to me, this large man, so careful of my belly, full of another man's child. But together we bring down an energy that I know will not leave until one of us no longer walks upon this earth. We are one now, the Calgach and I, united in body and in intent. We will do our very best for our people, on this land and in this world.

My intent is larger: I want the best for all involved, the Sons of Mars as well, while he focuses entirely upon the tribes, but we are the same in our hearts.

We lie hugged to one another for the rest of the short night. I doze on and off and dream strange dreams. I look around me as I wake, certain that someone else was within the Circle, but there is no one there, just me. Me and the still sleeping Calgach. So it was but a dream.

All feels good here.

All is well.

Onnagh looks at me sharply later, when she returns to the Circle just before the dawn along with all the others. I do not understand why she is cross this time as I have done nothing wrong. This is the way of it on High Summer. Even some of the married couples change partners sometimes. It is how it has been done since the time of our ancestors. But in Onnagh's eyes, it is somehow wrong for me. Is it because of Guy-us? I know she still sees my joining with him as a great betrayal. But the Calgach, now walking about and welcoming everyone back to the Circle in his usual amiable way, is one of our own. It feels as if Onnagh is just always cross with me now. The emotion transfers itself to whatever I am doing at any given time, but she is continually annoyed or angered by me.

"It is all Love," I say to her, for that is all it is, was, or can ever be. Even her crossness has this same source.

Before there is time for her to reply, it is upon us, the rising of the sun. It's coming, it's coming, it is here and we all raise our quartz shards high to catch the first rays. We will carry these with us for the next year, or keep them in our homes, over our beds, by our food, wherever the light is needed. This year, I think, more people will choose to wear these pieces of clear white stone on their persons, tucked into their clothes. We will have need of them. And there's so many more than usual. The raised fiery pieces of quartz do not only fill the great Circle; they abound in the trees and through the forest with the people, and it's causing a great raising of the light. And I love it.

I sit back on the flat stone, and a flurry of activity begins around me. The sun has been welcomed, and now people are bringing the food, so lovingly prepared earlier. Many souls worked together on this task. Old friends and new, observing, learning, and sometimes disagreeing on methods of preparation. But it is all in love.

The Calgach smiles at me from the crowd. He is smiling at where I sit, the flat stone having been made special to him, as it always has been to me.

As the feasting begins there sounds a terrible and great noise. I am shocked and shaken when I hear it, almost to the point of running into the forest to hide, but this is not an option for me on this night, or this morn as it is now. I am united with the Calgach in leading our people, and, like him, until the battle is done, can have no retreat.

But the noise is tremendous. And strange. It is like nothing I have ever heard before.

I turn to see from where it comes and find that it is: Jarredd! And others from Cullykhan too, marching towards us up the hill between the trees, with great, tall instruments. I had not noticed their absence in the Circle earlier, though I did note that Alara was not there, but I now see why these musicians and artists were not present. They wanted to make a huge entrance with this sound. It is not music that emanates from these pipes, but monstrous and ferocious screams of war, a warning to all enemies: we are loud and we are mighty. Cower before us!

The players of the instruments form a ring, outside the Circle, still making that terrible sound, and then they stop.

"What do you think of the Carnyx, Morragh?" asks Jarredd, as if this is a very important question, as we all gather round to see and inspect. He lowers it down so I can see, for it is quite as tall as another man above him when held aloft and played.

"You made this, Jarredd?" I ask.

He nods. "Myself, and others too."

The long metal instrument has a pig's head, and a tongue that moves when air is blown into the pipe. I can see that this tongue, just as in people, has given it a greater voice than a plain horn.

"I like its eyes," I say, tracing my fingers round the silver circles. "And its terrible song too. It is a masterpiece."

Jarredd smiles at my words, and gives what seems to be a sigh of relief.

"Morragh just likes everything she sees these days," snaps Onnagh, causing me to jump in shock at the level of spite in her tone. And she takes hold of Jarredd and whisks him away, away from the Circle, away from me, as if I might intend to take him too.

Carnyx

The many Carnyx continue to sound their warning cries throughout the feasting, with many people trying their hands at lifting and playing the instruments. These efforts reveal that it is a skill requiring much practice, both the holding of the heavy device and the sounding of it.

"It is good that we can become accustomed to the Carnyx on this day of celebration," says the Calgach by my side. "Then, on the day of battle, the sound will be a comfort to us, bringing strength and perhaps the power of this High Summer. Yet it will invoke terror in our foe."

The day of battle. He mentions it so lightly, the day of his death. He knows the truth of it. I know it. And yet he is jovial as we sit here beside the fire, in the centre of the Circle. Good company. He is. I am not, but then when am I? I may speak to people now, but really only when I have to. I am still the most silent of the Taezali.

I see Onnagh and Jarredd come out of the trees, laughing, close, touching, holding one another, and I am so glad. Jarredd has never looked so happy in all his life, at least not when I've seen him. And maybe this will bring balance to the strained relationship between Onnagh and myself too. I don't like her being cross with me. I don't like her constant disapproval. It feels wrong. There should be peace between us sisters now. I wait till Jarredd is busy explaining the workings of the Carnyx to someone again, and approach my fiery sibling.

"It is not true that I want all that I see," I tell her. "I would never take anything from you. And nobody could ever take Jarredd from you."

141

A frown passes over her pretty face. "Ach, Morragh, I ken. I am just not used to seeing you like this. To hearing you at all, even, maybe especially, on this night. Everyone else seems to have made the adjustment so easily, and I, your sister, your closest friend, still find your speech strange and alarming, and even a bit frightening at times."

"Because you have always worried for me. And that is the one thing I do wish I could take from you."

"Aye," she says. "But maybe it's also harder for me because I ken more about what's going on with you than anyone else. More about what you've been getting up to."

"Aye," I say, mimicking her tone. "I am glad about you and Jarredd."

Her face changes. Reading faces does not come easily to me; I have not managed the adjustment of looking into eyes so well, but I know she is uncomfortable with what I've just said.

"He's just a man, sister," she says with a shake of her head.

"Aye," I say again, and she laughs this time. "They're all just men, Onnagh."

She looks at me, and I am not sure whether she is about to be sharp when the babe in my belly kicks out so fiercely that it cannot be ignored.

"What is it?" she asks. "Is something wrong, Morragh?'

The babe fair dances under my hands, and I take both Onnagh's in mine and lay them on my tummy.

Her face changes again, and I can read and understand her clearly this time.

There is joy.

There is wonder.

"Oh, Morragh," she says. "This is a feisty wee girl. Like me." Her brow wrinkles. Thinking, thinking, sensing. "Aye, she is much like me. She will run about all over the place, with her Auntie Onnagh right there to chase after her and spoil her!"

I feel the wrinkling of my own brow, not so much thinking but sensing that this is not to be the way of it. The child will indeed be like Onnagh but... and I don't go there. I can't. I stay here. I stay in the now.

I take my sister's hands in mine again. "Let's dance in the Circle," I say, ignoring the finishing thoughts of the invitation: while we can. Let's dance while we can. Be happy while we can. Be carefree and joyful while that is possible for us.

So we do. We dance and twirl and shout, a bit like the wee bairns we used to be. And also not like them. For we are grown women now, and we are free, and we can be happy like this among all these people. Our people.

Soon Onnagh dances with Jarredd in a different way, and I sit by the Calgach, on the flat stone, in companionable silence.

And then everyone else, the whole crowd, goes quiet too, which is strange, and the light within the Circle changes. It dims. There's a sense of excitement. Like a coming storm... but not quite.

And then there's a clap, a bit like thunder.

And a bang.

And a strange man is standing in the middle of the stones.

We all stare at him, the attention of all people held by this new one now as I held it only hours ago.

As he starts to speak, I remember him, though he does not look the same as he did when I met him before. The exact change is difficult to define, but he is most definitely different, this teller of tales that the Calgach invited here. He introduces himself to the crowd as if they should feel honoured to be in his presence, and, indeed, they do seem to feel this way. I hear muted 'ooh' and 'ah' sounds about the appearance of this man.

He is now talking about the Calgach, and I am glad to hear that it is in glowing terms. And then, the storyteller is become the great man himself. How this can be I do not know, but he marches around the Circle giving orders just like the Calgach does. I look at the actual man beside me, and he is smiling.

"Crispus is good, no?" he says.

I look back at the prancing storyteller and realise this is his talent, his skill. He can take on the appearance and manner of another. He can be whoever he wishes to be.

And all at once, he is me.

I know it.

He confirms it as he flashes a smile in my direction.

"I will tell you a tale, a very great tale, of a woman who loved two men…" he begins, still walking and talking like me.

I feel shocked and shaky as I look across the Circle at Onnagh, and she is likewise infused with horror. Our eyes meet as we listen to secrets that were only our own, that we thought were our own, being thrown around this sacred space as entertainment.

Who is this man, and how does he know these things that he speaks of with such delight?

He tells of two leaders and one woman. This is not so accurate. Guy-us is not a leader. The tale teller also says it is a story from long ago, from the time when people raised the very stones we sit among now. And that feels true in the moment he says it, but his wicked and knowing smile in my direction tells me otherwise.

"And what should she do, this woman whose heart is divided between two men?" the prancing trickster asks, taking my hand and leading me into the middle of the Circle. "Perhaps this one, your Morragh, alive with us

144

today, friend to the newest in this land, and the oldest, can tell us?" He touches my arm, and I look down at his hand. He tweaks a strange plant that is wound round my wrist, and then I am transfixed by that, and only that.

I recognise it. Its wiry, hairy stem. The little buds. The creeping vines coming from it.

It is one of the winding plants that was growing in the great circle of the Old Ones when we visited. I have never seen it here in this place before. It was there protecting that special Circle. And it is somehow here now. Protecting me, from this silly charade, this play-acting that is taking place here in the sacred space.

I look only at the plant. I touch it with my fingers. I smell its green, fresh scent and think of the Hill Folk. And I walk back to the flat stone and retake my seat by the Calgach, a man of no trickery or charades.

"He must have heard about us visiting the Hill Folk," he murmurs to me, unperturbed. "It was, after all, not a secret."

The rest of the performance is a secret to me, for I remain in study of the plant, absorbing the knowledge it contains. I understand that it came here by human hand. The Hill Folk were here. At least some of them. Maybe they still are. No, they are gone. I know it as soon as I think it. They visited in the deep of the night. While the Calgach and I slumbered here on the stone together. They did not disturb. They did not intrude. But... they did something. I try to define what.

The nothing.

I feel it.

They did what we did in their circle. They went within, right inside the very stones themselves. With their minds. And then... and then...

I find I have moved. While deep in thought, I have wandered through the crowd and walked over to the great

145

recumbent stone and am now studying the remaining shards of quartz. Yes. The pile is changed from when I last looked on it. Some pointy white pieces are gone. And I am so glad for it. I am glad those dear, ancient people took something from our ritual. It was right that they did so. And it was right that they were here.

I cannot stay in these contemplations any longer though, and look round at the storyteller, Crispus as he calls himself. He is here, and I am not glad. He is here, and it is not right.

I am not the only one to feel this. His tale has ended, and he is now dealing with Onnagh, a very fired up and angry Onnagh. My sister is accentuating her words by pointing furiously at the ground and then at the storyteller. Jarredd stands at her side, nodding, backing her against Crispus. I love the two of them for this, but there should not be strife and argument here on this day.

"It is time for you to go," I tell the storyteller as I reach the group. "Your tale is told."

He makes a little bow to me. "And did you like it, oh, dark and mysterious Morragh?"

"I heard only the beginning."

He does not like this. His face becomes older, and a little bit cross.

"He must have been spying hereabouts," says Onnagh. "Some of the details, Morragh, they were too exact. About…" She thinks, carefully considering her words and those that might hear, even in her anger. "You know, some of our living arrangements. Private moments."

"I never spy," Crispus says, almost spitting with rage. "I told a story from the past, as you would know, had you been listening properly."

I put my hand on Onnagh's arm to stay her furious response and respond myself. "I believe you," I say because I do. This man picks things up from people. With

146

his mind. It is not exactly a power, more like a trick, a way of close observation. But he does not spy in a physical way. I add: "And I would like to thank you."

He looks interested now, tilting his head and raising his chin as he looks at me, preparing to be appeased.

"You drew my attention to this plant." I touch the stem that I still wear. "And it provided me with much information. This is why I did not hear the rest of your tale."

He's smiling again, more than appeased, back to proud and strutting. "Ah, yes, the magic of the tale. This is often the way for people when they hear my stories or even just my name. They are lead to where they are meant to be."

"But you do not belong here," I say, feeling it more strongly the longer I stand near him. "Your presence is some sort of farce... or pretence. You are the mysterious one, Crispus."

"Indeed I am! Indeed I am! And indeed I must go. But we will meet again, sweet, wise one. Though not in this tale. Crispus appears where he is needed, and I have others to visit now."

And then he is gone, and it is as if he was never here. He is forgotten, like mist on a summer day, like I know there will be later. And just as I think the thought, there the mist is. All around us. Thickening all the time as if to absorb or hide Crispus as he leaves. No one sees him go. No one notices him fade into the woods and disappear. But I sense it. I know. The others may forget his strange ways now he is gone, but I will not.

The mist does not last long. And it does not dim the merriment. Though we are all tired. We are all spent.

Later, as the bright of the long day finally fades, people begin to make their way to their homes and their tents, weary from lack of sleep. Exhausted by the antics of the shortest night. I ask the Calgach to stay with me in my hoosie. I whisper in Onnagh's ear that she should also invite Jarredd to stay, as I have already asked the Calgach. And that is the way of it for us, on this one night.

It will not always be.

In fact, it will never be again.

We all breakfast together around a small fire the next morning, sleepy and happy and content with bread and meat and tea.

It is the Calgach who ventures outside first, and so it is him that finds the gift outside the door and brings it within.

"It is for you again, I think, Morragh," he says.

The clay urn has flowers and ferns and tree twigs wound round the neck this time, held in place by the wee handles at the side. It contains more of the nutty oil, this one scented with herbs, a peppery, savoury greenness that I know I will love in food more than on my skin.

"Someone has been trading with Mars," he says, but not sounding at all perturbed by the fact. "This is their oil."

I feel Onnagh make the choice to say nothing.

Capercaillies

I thought there were a lot of people at the gathering of High Summer. There were. More people than I had ever encountered in one place. More people than I had ever met before in the whole of my life. But now, as we approach the day of battle, I know a bigger number. A greater scale. I need a bigger word than bigger, a greater idea than great; I do not have words for this stretching of a concept.

Many.

So Many.

Too many?

No, in reality, for the purpose of our amassing like this, there are maybe not many enough. But there are more yet to come. The tribes are congregating on the Great Hill. They are like a mighty ocean of people again, stretching for miles, right to the horizon and beyond. I sit on a grey stone outcrop, above all the camps and fires and chatter, distanced from the sharpening of weapons and the cooking of food.

I sit.

And I watch.

I take out my shard of quartz from High Summer, and turn the round rock over and over in my hands. It reflects the light of this place, and the brown and purple colours of the hill. It is beautiful, this stone, but how can it help us now? Maybe it can't. But people feel better for carrying these pieces of white rock, these remnants of the longest day and the shortest night.

I look down over the people, the multitudes.

How can it be that we are going to lose this battle? We are so huge an army. Though I was shocked by the size of the Roman gathering when I first saw it, from the inside of this hill, I have since grown used to large numbers. It seems to me that the Men of Rome have gathered less warriors than us, though more of them are still arriving too, as I watch from the highest of places on the Great Mother Hill. Some of the Sons of Mars arrive by chariot, but mostly they appear on foot, in large groups, marching in straight lines and then arranging their tents in perfectly straight lines too.

I know many more warriors are yet to come. On both sides. Day by day, there will be more.

Guy-us has told me this is so of Rome.

The Calgach has told me this also about the tribes.

But I find it hard to believe them. How could there ever be more – many more – people than this in one place? If this is possible here, how many are there in the whole world? My head buzzes with this thought, this question.

But I am quiet. I just sit.

I hear the capercaillies' plaintive cries from the back of the hill, the sound of those plump birds echoing off the solid rock clusters at the top. They would be wise to be quiet like me, or someone will soon grab them for the cooking pot. Many deer have already gone that way as the time of battle nears, with even the most modern of farming tribes returning back to the way of the wild hunt.

I feel this part of the land quiver in shock. It has never felt so many feet tread and march upon it. It is used to humans behaving in a relatively quiet way, a not to be caught in the cooking pot way, and moving around in small groups. It is used to the Old Ones. The Hill Folk. This part of the world is used to sun and the moon and wind and gales and rain.

Soon it will have blood.

Soon all will be soaked and watered red.

But I cannot think on that. That is not now. That time is getting closer, but it is not yet here. This is the time of readying. This is the time of preparing. The reality of war is not yet fully known here in this place.

"You thought I would not see you up here? On the top of Mons Graupius itself?"

It is the Calgach, and I look at him in question. These words – Mons Graupius – are words I have only heard from Guy-us until now, though he pronounces them a little differently.

The Calgach smiles and holds out a leg of something, some poor bird that sang too loud upon the hill no doubt. It is delicious and perfect. Just what I need on this late summer day, high on a rock.

"It is the Romans' word for the hill," he explains. "They think it looks like a hair comb, and graupius is their word for that." He laughs at the ridiculousness of this, then sobers quickly. "You must return to your house soon, Morragh," he says. "Before they come for us. Stay near those secret tunnels of yours, so you can get to safety."

The Calgach and Guy-us tell me many of the same things these days; the Calgach speaks here on the mountain, while Guy-us voices his worries deep in the forest. I listen to both men but will heed neither. I will be here on the day of the fray, and I will survive. Many Taezali will survive. They will be forever changed, but their lives will go on. I learned this in the chamber during the long hours of blessings given at High Summer.

I can only think that this is because they have listened carefully to me when I told them to run up the hill towards this crag and beyond to the Mither Tap when it is over, when they know it is time. But I cannot contemplate the matter much beyond this. The child that grows within me makes me dreamy, rather than critical and assessing. This

151

is good for me, it helps me cope. In my heart I know that while many of the Taezali are to be spared, for a great number this will not be so.

This ground will lie covered... but I do not go there again.

I also know that Rome is not going to approach us as soon as the Calgach thinks.

He is looking serious as he surveys the land and the people, maybe with some of the same thoughts that are in my head. I do not know. I cannot tell that. But I can tell him the one thing I cannot tell Guy-us. Guy-us does not suspect, does not even consider it a possibility. And he would try to stop me if he knew. Really stop me. I see ropes and tied hands when I think of it. But the Calgach? He may not like it, but he will not interfere with my will in this.

I reach out and take my friend's hand. "I will be here with you," I tell him. "At the start of the day. And at the end."

As anticipated, he frowns. "It will be no place for you, Morragh," he says, laying his hand on my rounded belly.

"My place is here. By your side."

He nods. "You'll be welcome, lass," he says in the voice of one also admitting something secret. He is human. He has brief moments when bravery fails him. But he never lets it show, never lets it affect his behaviour or his decisions.

And this only makes him the more brave.

To me.

I hold his hand tightly as we watch the lower parts of hill and all the people together. Higher up, behind us, near the Mither Tap, the capercaillies continue to sound their despondent cries.

Wee Fish

I am now as a wee fish in an ocean of bigger fish and whales and dolphins, and fancy coloured sea slugs and eels and starfish and pipe fish and octopi. For the tribes are fully gathered, and the tribes are fully decorated with their colours and their symbols. The symbols are old, of the Stone People and those that came before us, so far before us that I have never been able to discern or understand exactly what it is that I sense from these swirls and lines and grids. But there is power in them, and that is good. And that power is evident as the symbols are wielded and worn by the people today. They feel it. I feel it. And there is truth in them too.

Sincerity and declaration.

Identity and bravery.

This day of days will play out as intended by greater powers than us colourful wee fishies. And that has to be good too. Surely. Doubt has crept into the hidden places within me though. How deep that doubt goes, and how it will affect me this day, I do not know. The deep of that ocean is yet to be discovered. But how can a gathering of death, of killing and pain, ever be good in any way? It does not seem so now, and I believe it will seem less so later.

But for now, I am still in a dream, protected by the Goddess and the calm feelings induced by the child in my, now uncomfortably large, belly. That child, who dances often, keeping me up through the night with her musical revels, is quiet today. For others it is not so.

Onnagh is cross, and Onnagh is outraged: with me for being here, with Jarredd for being here, with herself, for what I do not know. Her golden curls twitch as she orders me to return with her to our house.

Now. Right now. No debate. No questions. No reasoning.

She can have her desire in one way only. I will not debate or question or reason with her. But I will not move from this hill until the doings of the day are finished, and they are not yet begun. I stand on the highest part of the crag again as I did on that quiet day, that emptier – though it did not seem so then – day, and look over the land. The Sons of Mars are lining up and facing us now. They are close. Much closer than they were before. They are right at the foot of the hill now. Commanders are readying their men for battle. I know Guy-us must be among them, but my eyes cannot see well enough across the distance to confirm this.

We are a hill full of people. They are line upon line, block upon block, with more lines forming all the time. But we, the tribes, are more. I am sure of it. Our swarming colourful mass is more.

Still Onnagh pleads. She pleads with me. She pleads with the Calgach. "Make her go home!"

"I canna make her do anything," says he to her, that day on the hill, and it is as if the words carry to me through the mist of a dream. I cannot be made to do anything. It is all my choice. All of our choices are to be held to account on this day, that day, a great day of days.

I see a creature approaching through the mist of dreams. A hauntingly beautiful creature. It is my horse. After I told the Calgach I would be here on this day, he got me this wonderful mare. She is pale, golden in places with wise brown eyes.

"Like you," he said of that paleness and wisdom, when he gave her to me back at Stane Hame. On a sunny day. On a peaceful day. He helps me to mount now, on a day that is neither of those things.

I climb onto her under the fierce glare of Onnagh who, though still furious, is now standing silent and resigned, stony in her rage. The Calgach has a horse too. A bigger one, a darker one, a stallion. We are to sit side by side upon them at the commencement of battle. I feel bad for my wee mare; this badness pierces the dream mist, for I know she will not survive the day. The Calgach's fine animal will. This is an easier thought, a lighter knowledge than that which I must avoid in this moment.

We ride through the men and women of the tribes, the Calgach giving upliftment and determination and strength with his words and his large strong presence.

People reach up to touch my hand, and it seems that this gives them something too, some sort of hope or strength, but I don't understand the fullness of that. They touch my massive armband, and the dragon one and even the dragon pin, for I have worn everything today. They call me 'Banduri', a word that means I am a spiritual leader of my people and now of all of them. I do not feel like I am this. Perhaps once. Now I am floating through the throng like a cloud, a cloud above a storm that is already brewing, about to break. About to change everything.

Everyone's world is about to be shattered.

The sounds around us are overwhelming already, sore on the ears. Many of our tribal leaders ride their chariots back and forth across the empty ground between foes. The wheels rattle and bang as they traverse the uneven terrain, making me think of giant hailstones falling upon a stack of wood, and then sharp edges of ice, cutting bare flesh, hurting and harming.

It grows close.

The battle.

The fight.

The war.

The Carnyx are louder yet than the chariots, hooting and hollering across the plain at the foot of the Great Mother Hill. I see the enemy twitch and shuffle in dis-ease at the noise. It may be they have not heard this sound before, or if they have, they know what it foretells.

The Calgach and I head downwards now, towards the front, our horses' feet sinking into overly soft and boggy ground now and then. The people part ways like sea water round boats as we pass among them, until we arrive at the front, and take our place between other people of import. I nod to Alara, and she nods back. I like this silent communication between us, and I feel something akin to approval emanate from her to me for the first time ever. And, I know, it is the last time we will ever communicate, her and I, here at the edge of the crowd.

Guy-us says we live at the edge of the world; our land is the furthest to be conquered, or for such an attempt to be made. And it is across at Guy-us that I look now.

I see him. From here, at the front of the people, the start of the ocean, I see him. I see a glint of light from some metal clothing that he wears. He is on a horse like I am. He is beside another man, a grand man, a strutting man. The grand man is also on a horse and not actually strutting just now, though he seems to be.

"It is the Agricola," says the Calgach, his eyes following the direction of my gaze, and then he points at Guy-us. "He is their leader. They say he governs all of Britain. I say: he can try."

My head swims, but not like a fish, more like it is full of seaweed and murky water, gone bad and foul smelling in the sun. "That man," I ask, also pointing at Guy-us.

156

"That man there, he is the leader?" If so, my lover is a liar, and I am shocked. And I am angered. For I did not discern such a great secret in him. How could he withhold this information and deceive me in this way?

"The man on the big black horse is Agricola," clarifies the Calgach, and my head clears somewhat, for Guy-us sits on a smaller brown animal. "Beside him is his bodyguard and spy. It was him we held at Cullykhan. More the shame he got away. He would have had much information for us."

"He would not have given it up."

"Aye, probably not." He pauses as he looks at me. "It's nae too late, lass. You can turn and make for home, or ride on up the hill to the Old Ones right now. You've given hope and power to the people already. Your part is done."

"I am where I should be," I say and reach for his hand which he gives with a smile. I smile back and know that this will be, not only our last smile, but our last connection free of woe and fight and anger and all the many disturbances of the day. So, I hold the smile and the hand for as long as I can there at the edge of the world, our world, our lives and our loves.

I sense a warm feeling on the side of my face. A surprised feeling. But then it turns fiery and confused. Shocked. Angered even. Things I myself was feeling only moments ago. So I leave the smile, and turn my head to meet the glare of Guy-us.

I smile at him too, but it is not the same sort of smile as I gave the Calgach, for a great distance lies between Guy-us and me now. He does not smile back. He is angry in so many different ways. I am here, with my big belly so obvious for all to see. In his eyes, to his knowledge, I am putting both myself and our baby in great danger. I am here beside the Calgach, declared as his ally, maybe more, he wonders more, and though he already knows of our

157

friendship, the sight of us together, and our closeness, has shocked him. The beautiful sunned skin of Guy-us grows pale, and his dark eyes enlarge in his face, as he looks across the divide of moss and earth and bog.

I hear the Carnyx and the wheels of the chariots and, far in the distance, up the hill behind, in safer places, the call of the capercaillies. They did not get caught and put in a pot. But we are in our own pot now.

I drop my eyes from those of angry Guy-us. Much will occur before we look upon one another again.

Mons Graupius

I was in a dreamlike state before; now I stand in the nightmare. I was in a soft and colourful ocean before; now everything is dry and hard and hurting and red. I had not imagined it like this. I had not thought of it at all, not in any realistic way. I'd heard a clash of swords in my mind and sensed the smell of blood. But I was like a storyteller, who lessens the dreadful parts to make them less harmful to those who listen. And I did not even begin to grasp the truth myself.

I could not have envisioned how it really is.

Not what it is actually like.

Now.

In this moment.

Here.

In this place.

It is truly too terrible to be realised all at once. It would take years of contemplation deep in the earth, down in the chamber, to fully understand and absorb what is taking place right here, right now, all around me.

But as soon as it begins, it is as if I am not a part of it. Nothing and no one touches me. There is clean, clear space all about me. This is in direct contrast to how it is for those around me.

Rocks connect with heads. This is the first violence. The noise of it. The smell of the damage done to faces and even the skulls beneath. I know I will never forget the sounds. Or the pain.

The, sometimes instant, death.

The, sometimes, usually, prolonged suffering upon the ground.

Then, the arrows. They come next.

Agony. Terror. Screams. Piercing of skin and flesh and bone. Breaking of bone. I hear the snaps amid the roar of human voices and horses' hooves and the screeching of chariot wheels.

No Carnyx now.

They are quiet.

The gap between foes closes.

I dismount from my terrified mare and let her run. And I just stand there. Here. Where I am. In the midst of it all.

Unable to move.

Unable to help.

Useless.

Battle swirls round me like a vision from the Circle, like a sign sent from the Goddess. But the time of visions and signs is over. I will know some more, big seeings, massive signs, before this day is done, and then I, like the day, will be done too.

All is changed.

All is ended.

Our swords are long and heavy. Roman swords are short and light. This fact does not go well for the tribes. They are cut down, scythed to the ground like a golden crop to be fed upon. I look into the eyes of Rome, and they look past me as if I am invisible. They walk by, slashing and cutting as they go, leaving many dead and maimed in their wake.

I do not have a long sword, or a short one. I have a sharp knife, given to me by the Calgach. He insisted I wore it in my clothing, secured by a belt, today. I knew then that I would not use it, but that my having it helped him in some way. So, it is here. But it is still, quiet, dry, unused. Harmless and benign, unlike all the other metal here on this field.

I no longer know if I am at the front of the battle or not. It seems to have no front now. And no back, no end, no safer space for people at all.

There is hand to hand fighting. Swords on shields. A dull sound among the rest. Thud. Thud. Thud.

Then: a deep guttural roaring.

Screaming.

Shouting of words and curses.

It goes on and on.

The sun grows high, so high over the boggy ground below, and I move through it.

I move among them.

The dead.

The harmed.

There is no healing I can give, no solace, no help at all. I am a thing without purpose, a floating wraith in this war. I did nothing to stop it, nothing to prevent it, when maybe I could have. I should have. I had the ears of both sides.

Bodyguard and spy.

Bodyguard and spy.

I did not know he was bodyguard. I did not know he was close to one so vital in this, to a decision maker, but I should have.

I should have.

I look at the ground between my two feet. There is flattened grass. Springy moss. And between it all, between all things now: blood. Everything soaked in blood. Blood that has leaked from where it should be, where it was doing the work of life. Now it is wasted and spilled.

I hear metal clashing.

No Carnyx.

No capercaillie.

No Calgach.

No Calgach. The feeling of the day is changed and shifted in his absence, and I move faster. I must find him. This thing I can do. I run. And then fall. I stumble in the slippery confusion and chaos of butchery. He was right about that.

Butchery of people.

Legs slashed and heads sliced.

There's a long shard of white quartz beside me on the ground where I have fallen. It's all bloodied and muddied as it lies in the wet earth. I remember it as it lay on the giant recumbent stone, newly smashed by the Calgach and I, this largest of the pieces. Shining with the last light of a beautiful day. A peaceful day. A day of celebration and hope and fun and joy. I look at it how it is now.

Surrounded by death.

Hurt.

Destruction.

I must find him. The man who broke this stone with me. The shard is slimy and cold and horrid as I pick it up. I want it to help me find him. I want it to direct me. It is sharp and jagged. White no more. I pick myself up from the ground too and continue to stumble and slip through the carnage.

And then I see him.

And everything is real.

He is real. I am real. And I have never felt such overwhelming sorrow in my life. He is pierced and broken. He is dead.

But he cannot be dead.

This strongest of men.

This leader of leaders.

I hear a howling. It goes on and on, like a wild and frenzied creature, a wolf or a fox; sometimes it sounds like an angry bear. It grows louder as the day grows older. It is me. I am hitting the Calgach, the body that held the

162

Calgach once. He must come back into it. He is needed. He cannot leave us yet. He cannot leave me.

"Morragh!"

I am pulled two ways like I never was before. For I will stay with the Calgach now. I will not go with Guy-us, bodyguard and spy. I wish that I knew the name given to the Calgach by his mother. He gave it up; he gave up this part of his humanity to lead, but not his mortality. Not that. What a shame, not that. How can it be, not that?

I am soaked all over in his blood. It is scratchy and dry on my skin and has hardened on my clothing. I manage to kiss him, my dear one, my Calgach, one last time before I am dragged away.

Two men of Rome have me by the arms. They find my knife. They take it. I do not care. It does not matter now. Then they try to move me. I do not help them in this. I do not walk for them. I hang and I am dragged. Guy-us is not one of the two men. He is the one ordering them. He is the leader now after all, in charge of these two at least. He speaks to me, but I cannot hear him. I will not. I shut my eyes and ears to him.

I am his prisoner now, am I not?

The thought is strange, new, wrong. I open my eyes to look upon him, Guy-us, the man I used to meet in the forest. Guy-us, whom I took back to Stane Hame. Guy-us, whom I rescued. He looks different now. He was always different, I just didn't know it. I refused to recognise it. I didn't heed my sister's warning when she gave it, and she gave it often. I closed myself off to this truth completely.

Guy-us as invader.

Guy-us as foe.

I repeat some of the last words the Calgach said to me now. "Bodyguard of the Agricola." And I spit in the face of this enemy.

163

"Wife of Calgacus," he says, but not in the angry way I spoke. He does not spit. He does not kill me either, though I am ready to go and would welcome the release of it here in this place of death. And then I know. I realise something here at the end of this terrible day. Guy-us understands that I lay with the Calgach, and the knowledge is hurting him. But I cannot care about that now. It is good that he knows. I did not mean to keep it a secret.

In the end, I do walk. It is just easier. One foot, then the other. Again. And again. The light of the day may be fading, but I see all that is around us. I hear the wails of the grieving and the pain of the wounded. I walk and am walked. On and on.

The camp of the Sons of Mars contains only men. No women. Except me. Just one woman. The place is full of tents like those we used at High Summer. Tents like the tribes stayed in. It is into a grand and big one of these that I am led, and then I am tied to a central wooden post. Guy-us tries to speak to me again. I close my eyes and do not listen. I will not hear him. I will not look into his face. Not yet. Maybe never. My heart is still full of the Calgach, and he is with me now. I see him with my eyes shut and then also with them open. His presence is not to be denied. He is not shocked to be dead, for he knew it was coming, and he knew it was to be today. He sees that I know Guy-us, but he is not shocked by this either. The dead are not as easily shocked as the living.

I feel his love.

His love is here.

Once Guy-us goes, I can keep my eyes open, and another man gives me water. I want to refuse but find myself gulping from the cup in great thirst.

The Calgach starts to fade. He is going now. Passing beyond. He reaches out a hand to me as he fades further and he smiles. I smile back, crying again, for him, for us, for me.

Guy-us is back, all of a sudden and loud: speaking, speaking, speaking. I close myself off to him again, all my parts: eyes, ears, mouth. I will have none of this, none of him. But then, in among the blurred and blocked off talk, I hear one word that I cannot ignore, one name that calls out to me in great pain: Onnagh.

The Golden Moon

Onnagh. I see her in my mind. I see what she sees. The back of a horse and its harness, the front of the chariot she has taken, and the land and sky as it whips by, darkened by night now and lit by the moon. The moon is a shock! I see it through the eyes of my sister, and it is huge and full and golden. It dominates the night sky, the landscape, the very world itself. Onnagh does not truly see the great orb. Her mind is darkened by grief and her thoughts occupied only with her plan. She is using the moon's light though. It assists her in her mission. I cannot see this, all that she intends to do, but I absolutely know where she's headed.

I am alone with Guy-us. I do not know his, or Rome's, plan for me, but it matters not, for: "I have to go. I have to go to Onnagh," I tell him.

I see her hands, darkened with dried blood, urging the horse on, faster and faster. What has occurred to make her leave like this? She did not run up the slope to the Hill Folk. She has gone her own strange way, leaving me on the field of battle. Or maybe she knows Guy-us took me. Maybe she saw that. I did not see her once the fighting started. I have no idea what happened to Onnagh or around Onnagh. Well, some idea. She is in shock. She is in trauma. As we all are.

But what, exactly, has gone on? I want to know. And I want to know now.

"Untie me," I order, and the Goddess is with me, that familiar power sounding in my voice, behind my words. She cannot be disobeyed, and Guy-us unties me. But he does not let me go. He holds my arm and whispers things that I know I must listen to now, if I am to escape and run to Onnagh. The truth is that I need his help in this. The fact infuriates me, but I manage to stay quiet and pay attention as he speaks.

I wait with Guy-us as he peers out of the tent door, until he says it is safe, then I dart off under the flap of the tent, to be on my way. He pursues at once of course, and catches up to me with ease.

In truth I am easy to catch, as I am immediately stilled by the sight of the moon. It is huge and it is golden. Its light is bright and clean and fresh and pure, so different from the land that it shines down on now.

There was nothing light or bright or golden about the doings of this day. The day that has been. The day that is finished now. The day that I must banish from my mind if I am to help Onnagh.

So I look at the glory of the moon. I try to breathe in its power. I realise that I have seen it look a bit like this before, and not just through Onnagh's eyes in my vision tonight.

On the night I met Guy-us. It looked this way then. And on the night of the day I met the Calgach at Cullykhan. The night of his blessing. His trial in the chamber. The prediction of his death. It wasn't full then, but it glowed with the same gold freshness and colour.

Tonight, those previous nights of the golden moon, and their events, are gathered in the air around us, and they will culminate and conclude... in something.

Something strange, and something terrible, more than one something.

I need this moment of stillness to breathe, to meld myself with the moon, to just stare at it and see it. To shut out all else. To ready myself for what is to come.

167

Guy-us does not give me time or peace for this. "We need a horse if we are to escape," he says in my own language which he has become impressively fluent in.

He is right of course. I need a horse, a big strong horse. I see it at once. Right in front of me. Agricola's beautiful black horse. The animal is unharmed, watered and fed, and it clearly likes me when I hug its head and stroke its nose and whisper that it is a good horse, a grand horse, and that the Goddess has need of it this night. It whinnies and presses its face into mine, the poor beastie. It has been traumatised by this day, like the rest of us, and will be as happy to leave this place as I. Though, of course, trauma lies in the coming events of the night. Peril too. For all of us. I may not know the details of what lies ahead, but I know this.

The horse is pleased to come with me, delighted and keen even. The horse is willing to serve a woman of the Taezali now, easily transferring its allegiance from the man of Rome.

"No, Morragh," says Guy-us, still right beside me, seemingly divining my intention.

"Aye, Guy-us," I tell him, untying the rope that binds the horse to a wooden stake, as I was tied to a wooden pole moments ago. I bend my knees and whip my body up onto the creature's back, then pause, clutching my big belly in shock at the churned up sensations within it, breathless and sore. "Goodbye to you now," I say to the man I once loved, the spy, the bodyguard of the Agricola.

"No," he repeats as I move off, the amazing beast obeying the smallest of commanding movements instantly. Guy-us is all at once up here with me, suddenly sitting behind me, which is most aggravating. Him behind. Me in front. But there is no time for argument. I know that.

We just have to go. And we do. Fast. Right through the camp with such speed that all those Men of Rome, the

Sons of Mars, hardly see us pass. They do a bit, some of them – everything and everyone is lit with a golden sheen from the moon – but they are not sure who or what they are seeing, and it will be too late by the time they work it out. They have seen so much today. Too much. Their eyes are tired. Their minds and hearts are weary. We will be gone before they know the truth of what they saw. Night and forest will have hidden us, and their pursuit will not hinder our progress in any way.

Ignoring Guy-us, I bend forward and whisper more information to the horse. He is a good boy, this one. He knows where to run and where to slow and when to take care, and he is heading in the right direction. We are moving through the far reaches of the camp now. We are almost out into the open, out into freedom.

But then the horse slows. He stops. Ears pricked, whinnying in fear.

I hear it too, what the horse hears, the thing that scares him. A whine. Then a growl. A familiar roar. I smell her. I know her. It is my Mother Bear. She is near. But how, and why? It seems impossible that her presence should be here in the camp of Rome. It is like a dream at the end of a nightmare. But it is true. She is here somewhere.

I slide off the horse, and then I just follow the noises. The scent of the bear has grown large from fear and abuse.

"Morragh! Either we go right now, or we will not be going at all." Guy-us's voice is low, here at the edge of the camp where we could be caught, here at the edge of his world, where we could be finished. But he follows on. He leads the horse, and he follows.

Finally, I see the bear. She is encased by metal bars. But not guarded.

Guy-us is whispering, talking, talking, that we must go, or we will die. That we must go, or we will be tortured before we die.

She is here. She is soft and warm as I reach my hands through the bars of her cage to touch her.

"Morragh!" He says my name in horror and in fear now, does Guy-us. He tries to pull my arms from the cage. "We cannot be here," he says. "Go, we must!"

"But we are here," I say, whirling and searching his clothes for a knife. I find a sword. A sword still sticky with blood. Blood that shines in the moonlight. Blood of the Taezali. Blood of the Caledones. Maybe even the Calgach. I pull the weapon across my face, taking the blood onto my own self, taking power from it, the power of my people. They give it to me willingly. This is their sword now. This is my sword now. And I have a better use for it than it had today. In one smooth movement, I pull the short and light blade of Rome fully away from Guy-us, and Rome, and turn, lifting it high.

It demolishes the leather fastenings of the cage in one blow and the great bear emerges, nuzzling my face. I have never ridden her before. Always I walk alongside, but tonight... she will allow this. Together we will escape.

I am on her back. I am leaving. Guy-us grabs at my leg from down on the ground. He seems so far away down there, so gone from me, so alone and part of the past in this moment. There is a pause, the smallest of pauses, and then he jumps. He steps off the edge of everything he knows and jumps. For me.

Mother and Daughter

We run together, we three. We flee. We escape. I cling to the bear's fur, lying down on her back, gripping with my legs as well as I can, given the size of my belly. Guy-us clings to my legs, and soon we are passed from danger and into safety.

I feel the shift, the change in our circumstances. And so does the Mother Bear. Once the cover of trees has taken us in completely, she slows, but she does nothing to rid herself of her burden. Without her, we would be slower. Without her, it would be too late.

Maybe it already is.

No.

It cannot be.

I will not have it.

I will not think it.

"Cullykhan. To Onnagh," I whisper to her and she hears me. She knows.

Swiftly and silently, we travel through the forest, Guy-us still not daring to speak, or to move, still too shocked, still too... numb. He is frozen inside by the day's events. It was not easy for him to be a warrior, to protect the Agricola, with me on the field. It was also not easy for him to walk away from his life with the men of Rome. But he did it for me. And he did it in an instant.

I reach back for his hand and take it, and we ride on. Animal and woman and man. Protected by trees, and the softness of the earth, and the strength of the bear.

And that strength is immense. I feel her shoulders moving under the fur in my hands. Her muscles are huge.

Her bones, massive. And steady, the whole of her is steady. She is my mother, my safety, and I know that her strength is in me too. I will need it soon. Very soon. But, for now, I rest here, I breathe here, on the back of the bear.

This is a break between times, between events. Major, huge, traumatic events. It is quiet here in the forest. Our progress frightens the odd bird, making them fly up fast with a fluttering of wings and brushing of branches, causing a shower of wee twigs and leaves to fall down upon and around us. But most creatures are asleep in their nests and burrows and lairs, and are not disturbed by our passing in the night.

The moon still lights us, now and again, through gaps in the canopy. It reminds us, or at least me, that something is coming. Something strange. Something as huge as the moon itself. Golden light will preside over everything that takes place this night, just as it did in the past, and all will be made new. What does this thought mean? I don't know. I find I don't want to know. I only want the break, the space, this moment of travel and quiet and peace. I stare up at the stars, made less bright tonight by the moon, but still such fiery little sparks in the dark.

Fire. That is in Onnagh's mind. It is her purpose. Indeed, she has always been a child of fire, but she is drawing on this power so strongly tonight. More than she ever has before. I still don't know how. Or why. But the time for that knowing will arrive soon enough, and for now, in this moment, I just look at the stars.

The smell of damp earth is strong, as is the musky scent of my Mother Bear. Any dark remnant of the day's travails that Guy-us and I might have added to the atmosphere are drowned out by these two, earth and bear.

It is deep into the night before we catch sight of the fort of Cullykhan. The smoke in the air tells me Onnagh is

172

already busy with her plans, and then the fire comes into our line of sight.

The great fort of Cullykhan is ablaze, red and orange and yellow against the starry night sky and the dark sea beyond.

Guy-us is concerned for danger.

"The danger was today," I say, urging the bear on as I would a horse, as I would have pushed the warhorse of the Agricola. This thought summons more thoughts of the day. "You were the danger."

"No, this, it is not true," he says, moving himself forward on the bear to better speak to me. "I did not betray you, Morragh. I did not betray your people. And in this, I betrayed my own. What would they do with me now? For this, tonight? Does this not prove my love for you?"

I make no sound. I cannot concern myself with Guy-us or his love right now. It is Onnagh who fills my mind and my heart. And it is to Onnagh that we go. And with great speed.

She is alone on the promontory, the high land of the fort. I see her silhouetted against the fire, arms held high, swaying. She is singing, I think. As I used to sing on my own. In my favourite place. Within the circle of sacred stones. But this is not like that at all. This couldn't be more different.

The horse and chariot Onnagh used to get here are abandoned just before the narrow stone bridge that crosses the stream on this side of the fort. I, likewise, abandon Guy-us and the bear and run on up to my sister, across the water and up the steep hill. My feet are quick despite the bulk of my pregnant body, despite my exhaustion and grief and soreness.

Those things are forgotten now.

Onnagh is all.

There is a new smell in the air, a smell like meat cooking, but different and wrong, so terribly wrong. And I now know what my sister has done. The fort has become a funeral pyre. Jarredd's body lies on a stone near the front of the burning building and is already being taken by the flames. Exactly how she got him up here, and how she lit the place alight, I do not know.

But I know she did it with grief.

I feel it. I see it. Jarredd's final moments on the field of battle. She was there with him. She held him close. And she felt the full force of her true feelings for the man. She knew her own love. And felt her life wasted. Their lives wasted. Time lost, never to be regained.

And, of course – Onnagh, dear Onnagh – everything was imbued with rage from that point on for her. Jarredd's death has caused her to own this love as much as she denied it in the past. And she is angry for it all. The past. The present. The future, gone. Stolen, even.

I thought I knew my sister's anger. I thought I understood it. But this is a whole new emotion compared to anything that came before. This is so much more. It is as if Onnagh herself, like the fort she has destroyed, is on fire and aflame with rage.

And it is with this fury that she comes at me now.

"You!" she screams. "Do you know what you did, Morragh? Of course you do! You always know everything!"

And she's on me.

And we're on the ground. And she's pummelling me.

Pain shoots across my middle. Liquid leaks from between my legs. And Onnagh, my Onnagh, who has always cared for me and tended to any hurt or need I have, does not notice.

She sits back from me and says in a flat voice. "I couldn't be with him because of you. I had to take care of you."

I shake my head. This is not true. Jarredd could have stayed with us. Onnagh's devotion to me has been out of balance for too long.

But now she is only grief.

She is only pain as she sits, crying like a small child on the ground.

And I want to take it from her.

But I cannot move. I cannot speak. My body has gone taught, and my words are silenced again as they used to be, as perhaps they always should have been.

Onnagh gets up. She staggers back from me. I reach for her, but really I know I have already lost her. My sister is gone from me forever. She is no longer mine. I am no longer hers. And yet… and yet… the bond is still strong, still in place, wrapped round and round us like cords of birth, cords of connection to life and sustenance and love. But it is angry now, that bond. Hurt and broken in places. Bleeding. But it still holds. I try to grasp this, this new way of being, but there is no time for contemplation here on this night. With my sister. At the great fort of Cullykhan.

Onnagh runs back to Jarredd and the pyre as Guy-us arrives on the promontory, the moon huge behind him, above the land, making silhouettes of us all.

"The baby," says Guy-us as he arrives at my side, taking my hands, helping me to sit, seemingly ignoring the fire and Onnagh and Jarredd completely. "It's coming," he tells me. "And here is not the place for the birth to be had."

He is right. He is right. My body is taking over, and this is all I can do now. The baby. The birth. Onnagh will wait. She won't move from her place. The fire will not spread outwards. The rocks will stop it. The sea will stop it. There is nothing for it to burn here but the fort.

175

And, I know where I have to be now: "The chamber."

"Chamber?" This word he does not know.

"Cave!" The words shout out as a huge burst of pain shudders through my body. I smell the metallic smell of blood. I have helped enough babes into this world to know that things are not going well in the beginning of this delivery. But perhaps they are as they have to be in this life. Yes. Yes. I hold on to that thought as I try to breathe. Things are as they should be. It may not seem so. In fact, it has never seemed less so. But this is what is. I breathe in deeply and push the breath out in fast jolts. I try to be calm and do all the things I would instruct other mothers to do.

Other mothers.

My mother is not here now. The fire has made her flee. But she was here when she was needed. She got us to Onnagh. And now, I think, standing with the help of Guy-us and pointing across to the sea cave, I have to get us to where we need to be next.

"You want to go down there?" He is full of disbelief, his dark eyes wide with it, and rightly so. Will I even manage? Well, if it has to be, it has to be, and I will.

Holding Guy-us, I manage to turn.

Holding Guy-us, I manage to walk.

And then I sit. Heavily. On the ground at the top of the cliff. I slide down the side of the promontory in my blood, leaving a red trail as I go. It mixes with other blood spilled this day, blood that is on my body and on my clothes. The blood of those that I love.

With Guy-us beside me, supporting me, I climb up the slope to the entrance of the cave, actually walking in my own blood now, for it has run down my legs and onto my feet. I leave a line of droplets as I go. The red blood of life marks my way through the tunnel and into the chamber where I collapse on the floor, with none to help me but Guy-us. A man.

I let men in here. I did this. I changed it all. But pain is all there is now and a desperate need to be free of this body within mine. It needs to be out! It needs to be free.

She is soon out, with no difficulty or complication, and she is asleep. This is what we say to mothers. Sleeping. But what we mean is dead. I know this is how it has to be, and that nothing will change that, but I go through the enlivening motions: the massage, the kiss of breath and clearing of nose and mouth. I cannot not do these. I have to. I have to know for sure. I do not trust my knowing in this moment as I once did. The Goddess and I are almost done with each other. This is another bond that is not what it once was.

Bonds. Bonds. They are being stretched and changed this night.

But Guy-us, too, needs to know all has been done to save the child, for he is in great distress.

I bite through the cord, and I hand the quiet wee body of our baby to him. He wraps her in some garment of his own, unwilling to let her go yet, so gentle with her small form. And this is good, for her spirit is near, and it wills me on.

The work of this night is only just begun.

Sisters at the Edge of the World

The spirit of our child is small and golden. She is flitting about looking at Guy-us and I, as we sit within the chamber. She is looking, too, at the body that could have been hers had she chosen to claim it, to stay within it. But I sense that she is a being of light, an old and wise soul, and that she calls me now to work towards a shared purpose with her. And it will not involve her returning to her body at any point.

My own body is exhausted. My mind cannot form thoughts properly. So I am operating on instinct only. I am being guided only. Sometimes it is better not to let the physical truths of the moment in. Not in their entirety. If we did that all the time, some things that have to be, would never be.

I am muddled, but I stand.

"We must return to the promontory," I tell Guy-us, who still sits with his child, staring down at her wee face. Her perfect wee face.

"Morragh, no," he says, as I head for the chamber opening. "We can take you home through the tunnels. You will be safe there. For a time." I see his own perfect face cloud with thoughts he has not had before, about our circumstances, and it is not the time for these things. Not yet.

"Me and the baby must go up top," I explain to him. "If you are not coming, give her to me."

I reach for the child, but Guy-us does not relinquish his hold on her. In fact, I see him hold her tighter as if she needs protection, perhaps even from me, but he follows along as I walk out of the chamber and down the tunnel to the cave.

"Morragh, you are still bleeding," he says, as we climb back up the side of the promontory, to Onnagh and the fire. Every so often he makes more comments about resting and drinking and eating and sitting and returning home. It is like the sound of the sea, constant and true, but not to be paid any attention in this moment.

My eyes seek my sister and find her at once. Indeed, no one could miss her. She is standing up on one of the great foundation stones of the fort. Beside Jarredd. Beside the blazing fire. Swaying in the breeze. She sees me and freezes. Another perfect face. Frozen beside the flames.

"Onnagh!" I shout over the sound of the blaze.

She doesn't reply. She just stares at me. I want to tell her things. I want to tell her about my baby. I want a different night. With different events. I want Onnagh to be happy that I birthed a healthy child who we will all love and cherish. But, unwanted as it is, the reality of stillbirth is here and my sister would be deeply sad about it, were she not already maddened by grief.

So I don't know what I want to say to her. And then, just as I think that thought, I do know. I know exactly what I want to say. Something I could not say before. Long before. But it must be said now. Here at the true edge of our world, truth must be known between sisters.

"Onnagh!" I shout again, walking closer to her, closer to the raging heat of the fire. "I love you! You are my dearest person in all of the world. Come down and be with me now. I had my baby. It… she…" I don't want to tell her that bit, and I falter, losing my strength, and stumble a bit as I struggle to stand in the intensity of the heat. And the intensity of the gaze of Onnagh.

She sways a little again, my dear sister. Then she smiles. At least, I think she smiles. The curve of her mouth is slight. It is faint and weak. It is not fiery like her. Like she always was. Like she always has been.

Our eyes are locked, us two swaying and stumbling girls, like wee lasses again as we once were. Onnagh draws an object from her clothes. It's her slice of white quartz from High Summer, reflecting the colour of the fire now, red and orange and yellow, sparkling there in her hand. She throws it down into the flames, tossing it away, her action and her face declaring it to be nothing but a useless piece of stone.

Useless like me. That is her message. I understand it. My efforts to prevent the events of today were too tiny, faint like a weak smile. Half-hearted even. And what could a piece of quartz, even one broken within the sacred Circle, ever do to help any of us?

Then, holding eye contact with me, my sister falls forward into the flames and onto Jarredd's burning body.

I scream and run towards her as well as I am able. "No!" Instinct moves my legs. Instinct tells me to climb up after Onnagh, and pull her from the flames. Clambering up here is much harder than I thought it would be, harder than she made it look. But something else is guiding me to leave her alone. To let her burn. "No," I shout at whatever aspect of the Goddess is demanding such a thing, then realising that Guy-us has my arm. It is Guy-us who is telling me to leave her. He is telling me more things I do not want to hear, like it is too late, and that I am endangering myself for nothing, and that she is already gone.

"She isn't gone," I roar at him.

She isn't. She stands tall in the fire above us. Still angry. Still full of grief. Maybe she does not know that she has passed. This is sometimes true for people who die in trauma. Maybe—

I am fallen to my knees in pain again. My first thought at the agony rippling downwards through me, is that I am bearing another child, a double birth, but tiredness causes stupidity, of course it is only the afterbirth. I catch the bloody mass and throw it across the rock into the flames where it sizzles and spits like a lump of meat. It is a lump of meat. Those that came before the Stone People ate their afterbirth. Yannagh told me this. She told us this. Both us wee lasses. It gave the women strength, she said, the strength needed by new mothers, the strength needed by me now.

Guy-us has backed off. By his stance, I can see that this is to protect the baby from the extreme heat of the fire. He is still behaving as if she is living. I feel so weak. Throwing the afterbirth took all that was left of my strength. But I cannot be weak at this time, in this moment. There are things to do. What things I am not sure, but then...

On my hands and knees, I scramble up the remaining base stones of the fort, of the pyre, like a crazed and ravenous creature. I crawl across the top to pluck a piece of newly birthed, and newly roasted, meat. It tastes good. And I do feel stronger. I eat more. This flesh has been cooked on Onnagh's pyre. On Jarredd's pyre. Taking it into my body is creating a strange power and opportunity that seems terrible and unbelievable when I first conceive it, my mouth full of my own meat. Meat that fed my baby. Meat that now feeds me.

But the face of this strangeness? It is perfect, like all the faces round me tonight.

It is the way forward for all of us.

I know this as strongly as I have ever known anything in my life.

Onnagh knows it too. Her disembodied spirit is looking at me with wide eyes and extreme shock, and quite a force of anger. Anger as strong as any she felt while living. Anger stronger than heat and fire and flame.

"Come on, then," I say to her, beckoning, encouraging the spirit of my sister towards me where I sit, wanting to know her thoughts.

She comes closer, but cannot speak in the form that she currently exists in. We have swapped our roles with this now, but I understand her perfectly, just as she always understood me. She fully comprehends the idea that has sprung up in my mind, and in my heart. She believes I would commit another abomination to correct this first one of her and Jarredd's deaths.

"It would not be an abomination," I tell her. "It is a natural and old practice. So old, it has been forgotten. But it is up to you, Onnagh. It is your choice. And yours, Jarredd!" I call out, searching for his soul, but he is nowhere to be seen. I sense that he can hear me, though. I hope that he can hear me. "If you want to come back, you will find a way. And you will find Onnagh again. She will be with me. And with Guy-us. If she so chooses now."

The disembodied form of Onnagh flares up in place of the fire which is finally dying down to charred bones and embers. Her fury burns bright as ever. Her flames are green and blue and purple. They are higher and wider than those that came before. Different. So different. I feel the skin on my face blister in the heat of my sister's fire but manage to stand up in the storm of her rage, and hold her eye in this moment of life, this question of life, as she held mine in death.

The flames around Onnagh increase and grow larger, and darker and then—

There is a bang, and I am thrown off the pyre and back onto the grass towards Guy-us. I can hear the rock under Onnagh crack and splinter, melting as if it cannot bear to be near this new fire and this ancient practice. My sister continues to stare at me, surrounded by the furnace of her emotions.

"I will do my best for you, Onnagh," I call, my voice too weak to shout now. "I promise you this."

And with that, she rushes forward to stand beside me, flames that are pink now encircling us. They are cool. I sense that this fire has its own perils, but it does not burn and blister flesh as the last flames did.

I find I have the strength to get to my feet and stand to face my sister. She pushes me, like she is testing me, and I stagger back but do not fall down. Then she runs. Round and round me first, and then... off to Guy-us and the baby. I run with her. Beside her, then behind her. We pause as we reach them. The man and the child, the tiny golden soul of the baby, still hovering near. Onnagh's fire is all around them now too, her spirit looking deep into the mind and heart of Guy-us, assessing, challenging, deciding.

He, Guy-us, the man, the father, looks only at me, his face dirtied by smoke and streaked with tears.

It is time. I reach out and place both my hands on the rolled-up bundle that is the baby, and it, she, starts to cry.

The Two Men

The baby is not an it. Of course not. It is a she. And she is angry. She is not so much crying now as roaring with extreme rage. The sound contains echoes of the pyre. Echoes of grief and exhaustion. It is the sound of Onnagh's anger with me. I hear her ferocity in it. Her exasperation. And her love, that has to still be there somewhere, surely? I hope it is. If it is not, everything that happens from now on is going to be so difficult as to be near impossible to bear.

Guy-us smiles his relief, his eyes lit with joy and love, good things that have not been felt here on this promontory tonight. And now, they come only from him, these good things. The baby and I, we are still filled with dark feelings. Rage and sorrow and shock.

I see the beautiful golden spirit of our child, the one that I carried within me, fade away now, just as I watched the Calgach leave earlier. And I feel such grief for them both, now, here, at what suddenly feels like the end of everything.

"I knew she was well," says Guy-us with a smile, his happiness telling me that he knew, as I did, that she was not well, or even living, all this time in his arms. "Morragh, we must get you both to safety. Down and away from this place."

He is right about this, of course. I have to put aside my sadness and go on. For Onnagh. So we make our way back down the side of the cliff, very carefully now, with our precious little cargo. A babe alive and loud is a very different being to one silent and still. She barely draws breath in expressing the great magnitude of her fury, the sound of it echoing all around us here at Cullykhan. The safest place to begin my new life, and my relationship with my new daughter, is in the chamber. So, surrounded by the smooth silvery slabs of stone, deep in the womb of the earth, I sit and nurse my child for the first time. There is not much milk for her yet, only the initial thick cream, and it is slow to flow. She has much to say about it, this angry little girl.

"You will get more later, Onnagh," I tell her, smoothing back her hair, which is dark now. Like me. Like Guy-us.

"Onnagh?" Guy-us has not left our side since baby Onnagh started to cry up on the promontory. In fact, he never left the baby's side. I left theirs. For some moments. I wander back into those moments now. Moments of melting stone. Moments of green fire. The dreadful moment when I saw my sister die. I saw her throw herself onto the flames. Am I actually just a person in shock, unable to accept the truth of this event? Am I inventing a strange and new story, from a half-remembered tale of old, so that I can feel I still have her with me, so I can believe that she is not truly dead?

"Of course she is Onnagh," says Guy-us, placing his palm on the side of my face, bringing me back to the chamber and the state of things now. He does not know what he has said. He means her name: he means, of course our new daughter should have this name, the name of my sister. But the ancestors, or the Goddess, spoke through him to me in my moment of doubt.

Of course she is Onnagh. Who else would be so furious with me? She quiets when Guy-us holds her, and we all curl up together and sleep for a time on the floor of the ancient chamber. All cosy and snuggled, deep beneath the stones that stand tall and true, high above us.

We need food. I know this as soon as I wake, and I know where to get it. It is not far. We walk the tunnel and climb the steps, and soon we are in our home of old, our wee hoosie. It is still night, but I know that there are other people awake in the rest of the settlement too, in the great round house. First, we must eat and rest and be very quiet. No lights. It is well that Guy-us likes holding Onnagh as much as he does, as this is the only way there will be peace. She wriggles and frets when I take her in my arms, or even think about doing so.

I fetch us food and we eat in silence. Onnagh sleeps. We go through into my old room, for it feels truly old now, old to me, old to us, and we all sleep there for a while again. We are awakened by the two arrivals I have been waiting for. One is an event. The other is a person.

The arrival of morning, quiet and pink and gentle, lights the house in a soft and comforting way, and we stir in our slumber.

And then the other, louder, but ultimately also gentle, wakes us fully. "Onnagh! Morragh!"

The baby opens her eyes at the sound of the voice and makes a noise, but not an angry one. I leave her with Guy-us, also awake now, and walk through to the main chamber.

Here he is. My father. My true father. Alaron.

His body, still dirtied by the marks of battle but unharmed, almost crumples in relief when he sees me. "And Onnagh?" he asks, surrounding me in a hug.

I feel confused as if I don't know what he is talking about at first. And then, I don't know how to explain, how to answer what is an extremely complicated question.

"She fell?" he asks as if he already knows the truth of this.

186

The image of her falling into the flames springs fresh and hot to my mind, and I nod. His face falls, but I can fix this. I can show him what has happened.

"Guy-us!" I call. "Come through. Bring Onnagh."

Guy-us does not have his battle clothes on now, but Alaron knows who he is at once, or so it seems because he draws a knife, and urges me to get back behind him. He has forgotten, perhaps, the knowledge he was given about the father of my child, and behaves as Guy-us did when first faced with the bear.

"No. No," I say, walking over to Guy-us and pulling back the cloth from the precious bundle he holds, so Alaron can see the baby. "This is Onnagh."

Alaron lowers the knife, and his face softens as he looks at the babe. "Your baby, Morragh. Onnagh. Yes." But then he is stern and wary again in the presence of Guy-us.

"Guy-us is the father of Onnagh, Onnagh as she is now," I explain.

A battle takes place in Alaron's mind, the emotions of it very clear to see as they run wildly across his face. I keep my hand on Guy-us's arm throughout this, feeling that it is as well that he does not choose to speak in this moment. He merely wraps the baby, Onnagh, back up, warm and snug. His actions are careful and caring. Alaron watches him closely.

"He cannot stay here," says Alaron, the leader of this tribe rather than my father now, in his leader's voice, then looking straight at Guy-us. "We will care for Morragh and the child."

It is an order. A banishment. And it is not how things can be, not how they will be. Onnagh chose Guy-us as her father. She accepted him there on the promontory tonight, or what is now last night. And Guy-us loves his new

187

daughter deeply. They should not be separated. They cannot be. Not yet. Not for a long time.

Though I accept something too. I accept the truth of some of Alaron's words. A man of Rome cannot stay here. Such a situation is not one that will be tolerated by the Taezali.

"I go with him," I say, then correcting to include Onnagh. "We go with him."

Alaron starts to argue, but he cannot win. It is what has to be and he knows it. I can see him filling up with emotion that he is unable to express in words.

"I know," I say, walking over to him and wrapping my arms around him. "I know."

He hugs me back as I press my face into his chest. To comfort me. To comfort him. "I would have you stay here," he says. "Have you raise the child with us..." He trails off, knowing his words are coming to nothing. "Morragh, I do not think you should tell everyone... anyone..."

Poor Alaron, his words are never to be finished today, for wee Onnagh starts to cry again, but the cry sounds different. I let my father go and return to my daughter who was my sister.

She is weakening. In her body. And in her resolve to stay. The energy of what we have done is more than old. This transfer of spirit is beyond what we know as ancient even. Its origins go too far back to be understood or known fully by us in these modern times. Perhaps the Hill Folk, the Old Ones, might have more knowledge about it. But they are not here to offer their wisdom. I understand enough to know that what we have done is not sufficient to tie Onnagh's spirit to this body, to this child of Guy-us and me. I take my baby, Onnagh, and try to feed her, to nourish her, but she is fretty and will not have any of the milk, which is now starting to flow better.

The men stand, silent, awkward in the presence of one another, but both watching me.

"Alaron, I need the ancestor stone," I say. "It is in my bed chamber."

He fetches it, glad to be released from the presence of Guy-us for a moment, I think, glad to have something to do.

I wrap the stone into Onnagh's blanket, made of a garment of Guy-us. It is not enough. Still not enough.

"Ancestors! Help her stay!" My words are a command which is not the usual manner in which the ancestors are called upon. I know I have to be totally secure and certain in what I ask, and in all that I do now. "If it is the will of the Goddess," I add, with absolute faith that it is. "And the will of Onnagh herself."

I close my eyes as the baby falls into a shallow sleep, one she maybe does not want to wake from. I feel her floating away, her mind swimming through the sea at Cullykhan. With Jarredd. He is here too. They are considering flying off together, to be united in spirit. But they have missed out. They should have had their life here in this physicality as a married pair. There was, is, much joy for them to be had in this. To have children of their own. To travel together. Yes. I see this. It is good and should absolutely be. It should happen. The babe needs to grow strong and tall and healthy and happy for this to take place. And she needs to start now.

Now. Now. Now.

Here.

Yes.

It is right.

And I know what has to be done.

And I know who has to do it.

"Alaron. Guy-us," I address the men together. "Onnagh and I... We have a task for you."

Daughters of the Bear

So. Onnagh and I are alone together. In our wee hoosie. By the forest. In the place of Stane Hame. Like we have been so many times before. And also, like we have never been before.

Whatever happens now, whether the babe lives or dies, we will only be here for a short time, and then we will be gone from this place forever.

So it is a time of cherishing.

I cherish the actual time itself, this break from activity and sorrow. Everything was loud earlier. Now all is quiet and still. Terrible things happened earlier. Yesterday. The worst things that can happen in the world. Now they are done. As I am done.

With some things.

Goddess things.

It is a new day, and there are new things to be done.

Then there's this place, our home, so full of love. Now and in the past. Always.

It is home.

It is home.

But soon I, we, will be gone, far gone from our house and Stane Hame.

And the people, the two people who are here now, they are the only two people who matter in this moment.

We love each other, Onnagh and I, regardless of all that has happened. Regardless of anger and death and rage and grief. The love will never fade. Though it will change, has already changed. I rock her to and fro, as I sing a song I remember her singing to me, when I was a frightened wee bairn who never spoke.

I am a new mother now, rocking my baby. Though this is not really how it feels. Not completely. And while there may be, nay, there are other truths here, this is the truly shocking fact: I, Morragh, am a mother. Another being, a very tiny and furious being, is now totally in my care. She relies on me for everything. As I once did, her.

I think about Guy-us. And I think about Alaron, as I try to get Onnagh to feed. It is not long since they left, those two men so dear to me, each eyeing the other uncertainly, set a difficult and unpleasant task together. It is such an important endeavour that they undertake. It has to be done, and it has to be completed today.

They will work well with one another, those two. A small amount of trust will form between them before the day is done. They will walk the ancient passageway, and pass through the chamber. Both have been there before, of course. In fact, they met in the outer cave, the sea cave. As prisoner and captor. But, like many things, that is over now too. That is done.

Alaron and Guy-us will have to work quickly before anyone else arrives at Cullykhan. Or here. Though here does not matter so much. Even Cullykhan will be safe enough for now, despite the fact that the fire will have been visible for miles around, and some people may visit just to see what has happened. Surviving members of the fort community will return in due course. But here, in the place that Onnagh and I sit, only our people will come, the people of Stane Hame.

They will stand beside me.

For now.

They will allow the presence of Guy-us.

For a short time.

But quickness is also needed for Onnagh. I look down at her pale face, eyelids so fresh and new, so different to those of grown people or even older babies. So pink and blue and perfect.

I stand up and feel dizzy, but it passes quickly, and I walk out of the wee hoose and into the larger place of Stane Hame. With Onnagh. As I have done so very many times before. And also, as I have never done.

Because she is new now. As well as old.

And I am different. As well as the same. I laugh out loud at my own thoughts, strange as they are, silly as they seem. But I do not laugh at the new circumstances. For they are not laughable in any way. They are serious. They are going to be difficult at times. Dire even, if things go awry. I know it, but I cannot think on it. I won't.

The idea to walk about and show Onnagh things to ground her here, to make her want to stay, seemed good when it sprung into my mind in the small house. But now that I'm beside the big round house, I find that I do not want to enter. I do not want to see the place empty and changed. I already know that so many who used to gather here for merriment and food and sleep, will never return. I do not need to hear the hollow silence. The bustle of the great round house, the way it once was, like so many things, is over now. The past is gone. And that just has to be accepted.

I walk away.

I carry my new baby over to the spring and the small spirit of water that is still there. I touch my fingers to the fresh, bright liquid and then to Onnagh's head in blessing. My knees give of their own accord, and I sink to the ground beside the shrine. Onnagh gives a small cry of complaint, but it is a weak sound. She is still fading. And suddenly it is all too much.

Ghosts of the last day crowd me. The Calgach. Guy-us too, though he is not a ghost, but his place in Rome is gone for good. Those who suffered and died, both the tribes and the Sons of Mars. Why did it have to happen? How did it help anything? How can it have been right for the world or any of us? Why did I go along with it? Why did I accept Her plan for this, her declaration of the Calgach's forfeit and the war won but battle lost? Well. No more. I am done with Her, as I knew momentarily on the field of battle. We are separate and unknown to one another now.

And I sob. For it all.

For my very weak baby.

For my very weak legs.

For Alaron and Guy-us and the task I have set them. This could have been such a different day. If there had been no fighting. If Rome had left as quickly as it arrived.

I want my sister. I want Onnagh to comfort me, but she cannot do that now. It is no longer her task.

And Jarredd, I think of good sweet Jarredd who loved Onnagh so. His gentleness. His quiet understanding. How can he be gone too?

It is difficult to breathe. My breath comes in gasps between sobs, and at last I calm to find the baby looking at me. Her eyes are focussed and her expression plain. I know what she is thinking. It was all my own doing. My choices led me here. Led us here. And they have to be lived with now. There is no going back. Crying over it will not help, though it maybe has helped me somehow. I feel wrung out like a cloth, tired and weak, but the old has passed from me, and I think I have let things go better.

This is us now, and we will go on. I say this to Onnagh and she gives a small sigh, but I think she is stronger. I think she is staying.

Onnagh. Jarredd. Onnagh. Jarredd.

I close my own eyelids and see the bones. The beloved bones of Onnagh and Jarredd. The two men, my two men, are there with them. Vision is not gone from me yet. Not entirely. Though it is not as clear as it used to be. It is as if last night's great golden moon has left a magical mist in its wake. I see everything through a golden haze now. I see that they are still hot, the bones. Still smoking on the pyre. The task given to Guy-us and Alaron is lengthened as they seek and find carrying vessels from the wreckage of the fort, and douse the bodies in sea water.

Good, good. I like that. The salt is right. It will add strength to the rites that are to come. The addition of male energy to this ancient process, the ritual, if it can be called that, is good too. Needed. So far it has really only been Onnagh and I that played large parts in this transfer of spirit to body. Guy-us was there of course, protecting the body of the child, but otherwise mainly only looking on, witnessing. Now he and Alaron are playing active roles. Not that they know entirely what they are doing. But they understand burial. They understand sanctity. Both men, both cultures, know and honour these things.

Up and down the cliff they go, those two that are so dear to me. Sweating. Working together. Bringing our two families together as must be. As is needed if Onnagh is to stay, and I think she is decided in that now.

Alaron and Guy-us wrap Onnagh and Jarredd in woven cloth to carry them. But as they descend towards the cave, the bones show some remaining heat, unfortunate steaming heat. So they are doused in the fresh and flowing water of the stream for a while. This is good. This is needed too. That small spirit of water, that is both here and there, will lend herself to this task, and add her power to Onnagh and Jarredd in their new states of being.

All the preparations are now in place for the sealing of this ancient rite.

It feels as if we do not actually wait that long, Onnagh and I. We are back in our wee hoosie when they return, the two men, and I can tell at once that they have been through much. They are both changed. They no longer doubt each other or glance in uncertainty. There is trust. Or there is a joint mission, at least, with much work still to be done.

In the end, all is simple.

The cloths the bones are wrapped in, from Cullykhan, from Guy-us, from Alaron, these are the right wrappings for them. There is no need to uncover them, no need to show them to the air again, no need to look upon the bones of the old bodies.

Guy-us and I, the parents, the makers of Onnagh's new body, carry the bones to the Circle. Alaron takes Onnagh. This is to be his time with her, and it is special. And I should not intrude.

So, while Guy-us and I walk to the Circle, Alaron, holding wee Onnagh all the while, fetches those of our people that are around to be fetched. I don't know where they were, or why I didn't see them, when I wandered the place of Stane Hame, no longer my hame, but still theirs. They were somewhere nearby. Watching me. Wondering about me maybe. But these people are needed now to see and to witness the internment of the sacred beloved bones. And they are pleased to see baby Onnagh, and to hear her name. In the midst of great loss, the newness of a baby helps.

The day is dull, grey somehow. The trees are still, no wind to move them. No rain. No sun. No golden moon. It is a neutral time, ready for anything to happen. And happen it does. I sit on the stone of sacrifice with my baby and watch everything.

Guy-us digs in the very centre of the Circle as the light begins to grow. Alaron digs. Darragh too.

Two men have become three.

Three to consecrate the blessed bones of the two.

"Onnagh and Jarredd," I say, again and again, at each small step of the way.

I repeat their names as they are laid in the ground, together.

And also as I pull my massive armband off and lay it in the grave with them. This is right. I know it. I feel it. I almost place the dragon band, made by Jarredd a very long time ago, or so it feels now, in there too, but then stop. No. It is for later. For what, I don't know, but that will come. That will come.

The dragon pin that Guy-us gave me, that I also wore yesterday, is no longer here, no longer in my possession to give or lay anywhere. It must have fallen on the ground somewhere in the fray and will be for someone else to find, in some other time. It, the pin, like so many things, is now gone.

Onnagh and Jarredd are covered over, together.

Together now. Together again. Together soon.

And we all sit together, the Taezali and Guy-us. And Onnagh. And me.

"Alaron! Morragh!" It is one of the old women who is speaking, exclaiming in horror.

I follow her gaze, and her pointing finger, and see the bear. My Mother Bear, come to see me again, come out of the woods to be present at this most important of ceremonies.

People are jumping up, returned to a state of terror again so soon after yesterday. Too soon. Weapons are being drawn by those that have them.

"It is alright," I tell them, standing with baby Onnagh. "She is mine. My Mother Bear. Onnagh's mother too. She saved us and walked with us and led us to Alaron, so long ago. It is right that she is here. We should welcome her."

196

People are unsure. But they stay where they are in the Circle. The bear stays where she is too, outside the Circle.

I walk out to her. Guy-us comes with me. Alaron follows.

I hug my mother with one arm, the other holding baby Onnagh. The bear is still full of fear from her earlier ordeal at the hands of the Sons of Mars. Her musk scent is strong, her fur damp. She sniffs the baby's head. All creatures understand birth and babes, for all creatures go through it in one way or another. New life. I know she understands life gone too. She senses it with her nose and her other deeper ways of knowing.

The bear and I and Onnagh and Guy-us and Alaron walk slowly into the Circle. The others scatter to the outside of the ring, still frightened, shocked by this new and strange occurrence coming so soon after the very worst events of their lives.

The bear bends her head at the grave. She walks to the stone of sacrifice, and then her visit is over. My Mother Bear, Onnagh's Mother Bear, lumbers out of the Circle with a 'grumph' noise, and is soon hidden by the trees.

Nobody speaks.

Two large bear footprints adorn the grave, the soft earth, and somehow this makes a tear run down my face and drip onto baby Onnagh's cheek. Again, this is right. Again, this was needed. The water. The salt. The love.

I say the precious names of Onnagh and Jarredd again as I raise the stone ball for the last time in the Circle, knowing it is no longer for me. My path, my road, is changed now. It is no longer Hers. And not even my own.

I get Guy-us to bury the ball inside the Circle, not in the centre where it stays sometimes, in the place where Yannagh told us it was found – Onnagh and Jarredd have taken that place of power now – but beside the stone of sacrifice, for that is what this is. I have sacrificed much

197

this day, and the stone seems the smallest part of it, but big in its significance.

The baby wails, hungry for food, enlivened again, and I sit on the stone to feed her. The people, somewhat calmed now, nod and pat her head, and mine, and pass from the Circle to go to their homes, or to move on, or to hide. There is still much fear in us, in the Taezali. I sense that they have had enough strangeness today and that my leaving, while still causing some sorrow, will be, in part at least, a relief. Normality is sought. Peace and calm are wanted now, not odd happenings with bears and Men of Rome and bones.

The people are looking at Guy-us as they leave. And wondering many things.

Soon it is only us four that are left. Me. Morragh. Who does speak now. Onnagh, who wails and screams as she expresses her anger again. Guy-us, who is quiet, and Alaron, who has questions.

Always practical, always caring. Alaron.

"We will leave straight from here and not pass through the big hoose," I tell him.

"And go where, Morragh?" he asks, brow furrowed in concern.

"North," says Guy-us at once. "Rome will not follow there. This place is the edge of the world to them. In truth, they are disturbed, even frightened by it. They will venture no further."

Rome. Of course. Both he and I are wanted by the Sons of Mars. And our child? Wee Onnagh? She would be nothing to them. Or a slave, perhaps. A child to abuse. We should go soon.

"I will not say you were here, should they come looking," assures Alaron. "Either of you. None of us will tell of this. I will make sure of it."

We need a focus, other than fleeing and leaving and parting, in this sad moment.

I point to the newly dug ground by the stone of sacrifice, smelling the cold earthy smell of it as I do so. "The stone ball will be found by the next Banduri. This is how you will know them. They will sense its presence."

Alaron shakes his head. "I think those times are done, Morragh. I know of no others who honour the old ways."

"Many have seen them this year," I remind him, but our conversation really only exists to delay what has to come.

As perhaps does my next request of the men. They take turns sitting on the flat stone and carve upon it the pattern of the sacred paths from our house to the chamber and Cullykhan. I add more to the design, knowing there is more to come and more that has been. The spirals of the Taezali are now marked here forever. For someone to find. For someone to use. I think Alaron is right. It will be a long time till this happens. I feel dreamy and strange as I try to see this, to discern who it will be and for what purpose, and so I stop. I am done here.

I hug Alaron, truly, tightly hug him.

And then we are gone, Guy-us and Onnagh and I.

Gone from Stane Hame.

Gone from the Stone Place.

Gone from Alaron and the Taezali.

The Beginning

I am numb. I cannot feel all there is to feel about all that has happened. I just mull over the facts about the people I love. I have left Alaron behind. I have lost Onnagh as I knew her. They were my most precious ones. Now I have little Onnagh. And Guy-us. And that is all.

And then walking is all we do. Then sitting. Feeding Onnagh. She is hungry. Still angry with me. It is still only Guy-us that she lets carry her, not me. She screams and roars if I try. I feel resentment about this. For all the truths of our circumstances, she is actually my baby. I carried her inside me for months and then gave birth to her body. These thoughts are all muddled through with the many other feelings that are starting to appear. And the resentment is building a stone wall between Guy-us and me.

I wish I could build a wall all round myself and feel nothing. I wish I could run away into the trees, until all has calmed and then crawl into my bed where Onnagh would bring me tea, and smile at my new baby, another baby, the one she said she would spoil, and all would be well again. And that no one had died. And that the Sons of Mars had never come here.

Yes, I would wish Guy-us away to have things back to how they were. Somewhere deep inside I know this is not exactly true, but I let the resentment course through me and push away the rest. It is easier than sorrow. It is better than despair.

I walk away from my past life as I did once before, and over the hill to where none of what has been can be seen or heard or felt. Well, perhaps felt. But there must be no looking back. I look forward only, now as we walk, and in time, we come to the far northerly coast and a brisk sea breeze.

And we walk more.

And more.

We go west.

We find a spring with a carved stone cup and I feel a spark, a touch of light from the water as I sit to feed Onnagh, watching the great waves of the sea and feeling their power. There is sea spray in the air around us, salt on the stone spring, built up over time.

The sea. The sea. It seems to call to me. To say: you are home now, Morragh. But how can this be? I am tired and I am stupid in my thoughts, and thinking things that are obviously nonsense.

Or maybe not nonsense. The call, the pull of the sea, has the same feel as the spring at Stane Hame. And the stream at Cullykhan. Though the water here is so very different from both those places. The spring at Stane Hame is not like the sea at all. It is quiet and bubbling and gentle, inland and away from the great expanse of the ocean. Cullykhan is rugged with cliffs and caves, the stream there cutting smoothly through it all.

This wee spring is very near the sea, situated on a gentle incline that heads down to the beach. There the land is flat and looks to be walkable for miles. The sand is golden with some stony places. I see grey rocks and pink pebbles. I feel the desire to walk down to the beach, to spend many a day on those sands. It is strange.

Water, water everywhere: in air, on stone, on our faces now too, and in our bellies.

Spring water.

Sea water.

All here.

All for us.

And then I know. She is with me still. The small water spirit. And she is no less powerful in being small and gentle. None of us are.

Ah.

This is left to me.

She is offering her continued power and companionship. But no burden of prophecy. Or mission. Just this one kinder aspect of Her. The one considered small and insignificant by some. She will be with me as I raise my baby. We will see her to adulthood together. And, then, after many years have passed, we will watch my sister, my daughter, so small now, head off on her way. But I will not think about any of that yet. Not for a long time.

I pull my baby, for my baby she is, closer as she sleeps now, full of milk and content, finally content.

I drink the iron rich liquid of the spring from the ancient stone and feel renewed. Somewhat renewed. Guy-us leaves us sitting at the spring and sets off to explore as is his way, his great talent in fact, a spark of vigour and life returning to him now too.

He is back quickly. "Morragh. There is a man. And he is in great need of help."

It is true. There is a man. A very old man, tiny and frail and close to death. He is in a wee hoosie a little way back from the spring, a little way uphill and hidden among the trees.

The house is smaller than the hoosie that Onnagh and I shared in the woods at Stane Hame, but it has similarities. It is the sort of place we are used to living in. Being in. Hiding away in.

Trees all around us.

Safe and secure.

So we stay. First to care for the man until he passes. Then, just to stay. We wonder if we have travelled far enough to be safe. But we are the new keepers of the ancient spring now. This is our identity, and travellers to the place accept us without question. There is no community here like there was at Stane Hame. There is no one here to question our arrival. It is just us. And that is how it needs to be.

Guy-us never speaks in front of the people who pass this way. If they were to hear his speech, they would know he was of Rome, or at least from some other place, and that cannot be known. Not here. Not now.

I am the one who speaks to people. Me. Morragh. Who never spoke. I am the woman with the mute mate and the beautiful baby. People love to see baby Onnagh and to speak to her and generally adore and admire her.

It seems we are liked here. Offerings of food and coins are regularly left at the spring, and with these we live simply by the sea. The house is just one small round room, but we manage very well.

News reaches us through the many visitors to the spring. We hear of the great battle on the hill that the Romans call Mons Graupius. We hear how the Sons of Mars were disturbed by the number of bodies on the field of war after that day was done. There had been so many more living bodies earlier. Where did they all go? It was as if they melted into the very land itself. And of course, in a way, they did.

"I hear the people were saved by those that live within the hill," I tell the visitors. "The Hill Folk, the Old Ones, led the survivors through their secret tunnels and passageways to safety." And I hope that those dear people do live on in story and legend as they wished.

Once, I think, but I am not completely sure, the teller of tales visits, the man who caused so much consternation

203

during that last High Summer at Stane Hame. He looks different now, and he does not appear to recognise me, which is good. In fact, he hardly looks at me. His attitude appears to be that it is an honour for us to offer him water, and that makes me all the more sure that it is him. Neither of us mention our previous meeting, if, indeed, he remembers it, and that is well too.

The sea here sometimes makes me think strongly of Cullykhan. The flames of the fire in our wee house do too. But less often as time goes on.

Because Onnagh.

She is my world now.

And she is a small wildling. Running everywhere. In among everything and everyone. People like me well enough, but they adore Onnagh. Returning travellers ask after her, hoping to see her, and bring her gifts of toys and cakes and cloth. She delights in it all.

And she takes all from me.

All my strength.

All my love.

All my time.

As I once did, her.

The years pass, and more news comes of the world beyond the spring from those who travel this way. The Sons of Mars leave, as I knew they would. They march south again, giving up their quest to control the tribes. The tribes cannot be controlled, not governed as Rome would have them be. Onnagh listens to all this news as it arrives and says nothing as if she does not really understand. But somewhere deep down, I know she does understand. She knows some truth. She feels the import of the event.

And the land relaxes. The air is peaceful again. The hills and the valleys and the sea and the beach, and even the sky are changed, different. Freedom is here. Freedom from oppression. Freedom from governance, or attempted governance. It is come, just as the Calgach wanted, just as he paid for.

Onnagh grows into a beautiful young woman, as her parents grow older. Guy-us has grey hairs now, just a few, dotted around his head.

He spends a lot of time – years – improving the shelter over the spring. The building he eventually creates is unusual looking, domed in a way I have not seen before except in dreams and visions. I think he has built a small temple in the style of the Sons of Mars.

"I have not, Morragh," he assures me. "I have kept it simple."

But in one sense, it is not simple. He has aligned the doorway to the rising of the sun at the equinox, in both spring and autumn. For me. And for Onnagh. We may not have our stones here, but we are blasted by a beam of magical light through the opening twice a year. Even when it is cloudy, it feels so special. Like a gift. Which, of course, it is.

And then the day finally comes. It dawns frosty as I light the fire for tea and food. I hear laughter from down by the spring. Onnagh. And the deep voice of a man. It is not Guy-us, as he is here, still sleeping in bed. It is a young man that Onnagh laughs with. I catch sight of him before he is gone. He has a shock of bright hair and, once he has left, I hear Onnagh humming happily to herself as she gathers wild garlic for the soup we will eat later.

The young man comes again, and again, day after day. Though I never meet him. Onnagh keeps him hidden away from me, in some old understanding, or misunderstanding, of a past she will not repeat. It is sad. I would have liked to know him a little. To see who my daughter is going to spend her days and her life with.

Because I know this is who he is, the young man. And it is not just with my inner sense that I discern this truth.

205

One day, I hear Onnagh tell Guy-us that the young man has a grand plan to travel south and maybe even further afield. Maybe even across the sea. He wants to build his business and there are more people in southern places to be customers than in this corner of the world. Guy-us confirms that this last part is true.

I hear admiration in Onnagh's voice as she tells of the plan, and excitement. And I know – I absolutely know – that she has been invited to go too. And that she will accept.

But of course, I remind myself, I do know this man. I know exactly who he is. He is a good and caring soul, born to be with Onnagh, my baby, my sister, my Onnagh.

I remember the gentle wisdom of Jarredd. I recall him asking: "Does it make you happy, Morragh, speaking like this now?" and how he was the only one to ask this. I could answer him now. The answer, after all these years, is yes. I like speaking to the visitors to the spring. I enjoy our, usually, simple conversations, using this easy and basic form of communication.

I enjoyed my days of not speaking too, in the past. That deep focus on other things, inner things, visions, intense knowings. Neither way is better. Neither way is worse. Things were as they were, and are as they are, as is needed in life. And now, I speak. And it does make me happy.

Then one day, my daughter speaks to me. Really speaks to me, as she has never done before. Always it was Guy-us she confided in, Guy-us she laughed with, Guy-us she smiled with.

"Stane Hame," she says, having come up the hill to where I am sitting on a stone among the trees. I saw her slim, dark form weaving between them. Gracefully. Elegantly, how she always moves. This aspect of Onnagh comes from Guy-us. He says she carries herself like his mother always did. So, our daughter holds a little of Rome in her body. And, like the rest of her, it is beautiful.

"Is it real?" she asks now, standing before me. "Is Stane Hame a real place?"

I smile. "Yes, Onnagh. Stane Hame is very real."

"I must have heard you and father speak of it."

"Maybe." But I do not think so. I am sure we have never spoken of it since we came to live here.

"I think I should visit it, them, the people there."

"They would love that, I am sure," I say, not really being sure at all. Who will still be there? Alaron, I think. I may not have the gifts of the Goddess now, but surely I would have sensed if he had passed. He would have visited, if only in a dream. And on that day of blessings in the chamber, so long ago now, I foresaw a long life for him, peaceful at the end.

"I'm sorry," she says.

"Onnagh, you have nothing to—" I start to say, but then I let her finish. She needs to speak out her truth.

"I have always felt so angry."

I know she means with me. "I know."

"But I do love you. Really, I do." There's a pause, and she sits down on the stone beside me. "Mother."

And then we are hugging. And crying. And I am so glad that she gave me this gift before... before she goes. Mother. She's never said it before. And it is mine now. My name. My title. Forever.

Guy-us speaks to the young man many times. He puts aside any fear of being found out as a man of Rome and interrogates him. He finally concludes that the man is suitable for our Onnagh, and that he can provide well for the two of them with his wares. His jewellery and other items are of fine quality, and he has good knowledge and business ideas.

207

I smile when I hear of the jewellery. But I do not go near. I hide away in the trees when he visits. I will not involve myself in Onnagh's new life in any way. This is how it has to be. And in the end, it does not hurt as much as I thought it would.

I give Onnagh the dragon band that Jarredd made for me. I slide it up her arm as Guy-us slid it up mine that very first night in the Stone Circle. She likes it, I can see. She is keen to show it to the young man.

I have heard his name, this new man of Onnagh's, but I never think it. To me he is Jarredd, and he is the young man. I don't want to know any more. I don't want to hear or see any more than that.

And then, it is time. It has been many years in the coming, but it still feels too soon.

Guy-us only just manages to hold back his tears until she is gone. She looks back at me before she turns to finally leave, and for the first time since she came into this life, we share a fully unguarded smile. We have understanding. We have love.

She is free now.

And so are we.

I put my arms round Guy-us, feeling the wall that has existed between us for so long crumble away into dust at our feet, and my love for him bursts back out and all over the place again.

"We will have another, Guy-us," I tell him, and he turns his head to look at me in disbelief, for our way of being together since little Onnagh came to life there on the great promontory of Cullykhan, has not been a way that would bring any more children into this world.

"Oh Aye," I assure him. "Onnagh's started on her new path now, free of burden, free to be happy, and so are we. This is the beginning we've all been waiting for, working towards for so long."

And I take his hand and lead him up the hill, beyond the spring, beyond our house, and to the rest of our life together.

Historical Notes

There is little definite information about the ancient Taezali tribe of northern Scotland, other than a mention by the geographer Ptolemy as he mapped Britain. I've chosen to refer to the people as Taezali and the lands as Taexali as this seems to be what Ptolemy was doing. Taexalon Promontory, or Taexali point, is thought to be either Kinnaird Head in Fraserburgh or Rattray Head a little further down the eastern coast. The tribe's response to the invasion of Agricola and his forces is unknown.

The Calgach, or Calgacus, is the first Caledonian ever described in history, and this was done by the Roman historian Tacitus. Aspersions have been cast against the accuracy of much that Tacitus wrote. Agricola was his father-in-law, and his adoration of the man does seem to have been somewhat sycophantic. However, I find his writing to be very human and relatable and have used his account of the battle in my descriptions. He wrote an astonishing, and admittedly unbelievable, pre-battle speech for Calgacus, which I borrowed a little from too. The name of Calgacus is possibly derived from the Celtic 'calg-ac-os' meaning sword and may be linked to the Gaelic 'calgach' which translates as prickly and fierce.

The great circles of the Hill Folk are based on the stone circle found at Loanhead of Daviot, and the remains of another circle across the valley from it. Morragh's Circle is inspired by the stones of Aikey Brae. White quartz fragments have been found by archaeologists in many of the recumbent circles of Aberdeenshire. I chose to ascribe them a ritualistic use. Also found in and near to some circles are the mysterious stone balls, often intricately carved. Their usage is unknown, weaponry being ruled out by the fact they show no wear and tear. They're beautiful objects and certainly worth a quick Google Images search.

The massive jewellery presented to Morragh and the Calgach is real too, and these stunning objects have been found in Aberdeenshire.

Bennachie is the Great Mother Hill, though there is argument about where Mons Graupius, as the Romans called it, was actually located. There are a few claims to it. I think the description fits Bennachie well, and the fact that there was an enormous Roman marching camp at nearby Durno at the right time, supports this.

Over two hundred of Scotland's Bronze and Iron Age hill forts, including the one at Cullykhan Bay, are vitrified, meaning that at some point the stone reached temperatures so high that it melted. It's a bit of a mystery, and my little story is certainly not attempting to offer an explanation. Theories on what caused the vitrification of these forts range from fires occurring during battle, to ingenious construction methods and even alien invasion!

The spring where Morragh and Guy-us go at the end of the book is based on the Red Well near the village of Whitehills in Aberdeenshire. There is local folklore linking the beehive shaped building over the spring to visiting Romans in the ancient past. It's said to be aligned to the rising of the sun on the equinox, in both spring and autumn. It's also said to be haunted by an old lady witch. I was once locked in the domed hoosie as a child to see if the witch would get me. She didn't.

Acknowledgements

This book took seven years to write. For some of that time, I was so ill that I could hardly walk. But I could type. However, later I found that much of that work had to go. My brain had apparently been as weak as my body. Then my earlier historical books got published, and I had to lay 'Sisters' aside to edit those. Finally, I dug out the neglected manuscript, polished and polished, cried a copious amount of tears over Morragh and Onnagh's story, and decided it was time to let it fly out into the world.

As ever, huge thanks go to my family for their endless support. To everyone who advised me on the writing and publication of this book, thank you too. To my Kofi supporters, your help has been hugely appreciated.

And to my neurodiverse brothers and sisters across the world: our ways are varied and many. I hope I've done us justice here in this tale.

Author Bio

Ailish Sinclair trained as a dancer and taught dance for many years, before working in schools to help children with special needs. A short stint as a housekeeper in a castle fired her already keen interest in untold stories of the past, and she sat down to research and write.

She now lives beside a loch with her husband and two children where she writes and dances (yes, still, when her chronic medical conditions allow, pah!) and eats rather a lot of chocolate.

More Ailish

www.ailishsinclair.com

@AilishSinclair on Twitter and Instagram

Sign up for the newsletter at ailishsinclair.com

Printed in Great Britain
by Amazon